A MOST SUITABLE BRIDE: A REGENCY ROMANCE

LANDON HOUSE (BOOK 5)

ROSE PEARSON

A MOST SUITABLE BRIDE

PROLOGUE

"Lady Hayward?"

Stepping into the Duke's study, Lady Hayward lifted her eyes to the gentleman before her, finding herself more comfortable in his presence than she had in the past. They had begun to form a closer acquaintance these last few years and she had been grateful for his help with her sons. He had aided her eldest, the recently titled Lord Hayward, in all of his duties and in matters of business. Her younger son was also being instructed and guided in matters of business, meaning that she herself had no concerns as regarded her sons' futures. With the Duke of Landon guiding them, she had every confidence that they would do very well indeed. In return, of course, she had been charged with assisting the Duke's daughters to find suitable matches and, thus far, had been quite successful.

However, Lady Maria was proving something of a concern, it seemed.

"I thank you for coming," the Duke began, waving

her towards a chair as he himself rose from behind his large mahogany desk and came towards her, before easing himself into a large, comfortable looking chair that was a little closer to the fire. It was almost spring by now, of course, but the evenings could still be a little chilly.

"But of course," Lady Hayward replied, quickly. "You know that I have been very glad to assist with Lady Maria these last two weeks. She is fully prepared to return to London with me now."

The Duke nodded, although his green eyes glittered with doubt.

"She has," he said, slowly, "already enjoyed one spring Season. And thereafter, was in London prior to Christmas."

Lady Hayward nodded, spreading her hands.

"I am aware of that, Your Grace," she answered quietly, understanding now that the Duke's concern was that Lady Maria might not find a suitable match. "However, last Season she was simply acquainting herself with London and the *beau monde*. There is, of course, a great deal to take in."

"And during the winter months?"

Lady Hayward allowed herself a small shrug.

"London is quieter then," she stated plainly, although she knew full well that such a thing had not prevented Lady Charity from securing an excellent match. "It might simply be that the gentlemen who were expected to be present simply were not."

After a moment, the Duke let out a long, heavy sigh and shook his head. Then he settled his elbows on the arms of his chair and pressed his fingertips together to make an arch, looking at her steadily over the top of them. Lady Hayward shifted a little in her chair, feeling somewhat unsettled at the scrutiny she was presently under, beginning to fear that the Duke was concerned that *she* might be the reason for his daughter's lack of success.

"Lady Hayward," he continued, his tone rather practical. "I would have you be truthful with me."

She nodded.

"But of course."

"My daughter is…" His eyes flicked to one side of the room as he searched for the right words to say. "She is a little different from her sisters." Resisting the urge to ask what such a statement meant or, in fact, to disagree with it as she wished, Lady Hayward wisely chose to remain silent. "She is a bluestocking," he continued, bluntly. "There is no hiding it. She has read a great deal and is very intelligent indeed." A small, somewhat indulgent smile pulled at his lips. "I will not pretend that I have prevented her from becoming so, although perhaps I ought to have done."

"I do not think that you would have been right in such a thing, Your Grace," she replied, swiftly. "There is nothing improper about a young lady having intelligence and wit."

"But if she does nothing *but* read, learn and explore all manner of things, instead of fixing her concentration on painting, the pianoforte and the like, then surely that will make the gentlemen of the *ton* less inclined towards her!"

Lady Hayward hesitated, biting her lip for a moment as she clasped her hands tightly together. There was truth in the Duke's statement, but she did not want to admit it aloud. To do so would be to imply that there was something wrong with Lady Maria, something which went against her when, as far as Lady Hayward herself was concerned, to be an avid reader and to know a very great deal indeed was nothing short of wonderful.

"It may push aside *certain* gentlemen," she said, speaking with great consideration as she weighed up every word. "But, as with your other daughters, I am eager for Lady Maria to be courted and, indeed, to wed a gentleman who values her highly. That gentleman will, of course, be aware of her bluestocking tendencies and will either accept them or be glad of them. I should not like Lady Maria to be wed to a gentleman who would discourage her in such things!"

The Duke nodded thoughtfully, although his gaze remained fixed upon her. Lady Hayward resisted the urge to shift in her chair, knowing that the Duke was only considering what was best for his daughter. Despite the fact that he had been less than involved in his daughters' lives, Lady Hayward knew that he cared deeply for each of them, but expressed it in his own way.

"Might I ask, Lady Hayward, whether or not you believe such a gentleman might be found for Maria?"

Her answer was immediate and she spoke without hesitation or delay.

"I am absolutely certain that Lady Maria will secure a suitable gentleman, Your Grace," she stated, firmly. "It may take a little longer, but it is, as far as I am concerned, utterly without question."

This, it seemed, was what the Duke had been waiting

to hear. His features began to relax, his brow was no longer furrowed and the questioning look faded from his eyes.

"Then I shall pray that this Season will be Lady Maria's success," he replied, rising from his chair and indicating, by doing so, that their conversation was now quite at an end. "Thank you, Lady Hayward. You have calmed my worries a great deal."

"I am glad to have been able to do so," she answered, honestly. "If there is anything else, Your Grace?"

He gave her a wave of his hand, only to press his hand to his heart and incline his head. When he lifted it and looked back at her, she was surprised to note a look of embarrassment flitting across his features. Perhaps he had realized just how dismissive the gesture had been, and Lady Hayward found herself rather touched that he would, thereafter, think to silently apologize.

"No, Lady Hayward, that is all," he said, as she dropped into a quick curtsey. "Good evening."

"Good evening," she replied, before making her way to the door and leaving the room.

CHAPTER ONE

"There is less excitement this year, I think."

Lady Hayward nodded in understanding as Lady Maria Forrest looked out of the window once more, her heart no longer as eager nor as delighted as it had been last Season. London was, of course, very exciting indeed, and she was certainly looking forward to all that the Season would hold. However, were she to admit it aloud, Maria would state that she was a little afraid that this Season would prove to be as disappointing for her as the last. She had not made a particular impression upon the *beau monde* and when she had been in conversation, she had found the ladies less than eager to continue speaking with her and some of the gentleman rather bemused. Yes, there had been dancing and the like, and she had made a good many acquaintances but there had not been any overt interest from any of the gentlemen of London. It had been the very same during the autumn and winter months when she had been in London with Lady Hayward, and Maria was beginning to worry that she would not make a match. Would she become the spinster of the family? The maiden aunt who had to rely on her sisters for grace and kindness towards her?

"You need not worry, Lady Maria." Maria started violently, looking to see Lady Hayward smiling at her gently, evidently aware of all that Maria had thought, without her having to say a word. "I can tell by your expression that you are concerned over what might occur this Season, but I am quite certain that all will go well."

Maria's smile was a little tight.

"It seems I have not done as well as my sisters."

She did not want to tell Lady Hayward that she had overheard a little of the conversation between her and the Duke, and that now she was fully aware of her father's concern that she would not find a suitable match – although at least, it seemed that Lady Hayward did not share such a concern - which was something of a relief.

Lady Hayward let out an exclamation and sliced the air with her hand.

"My dear Lady Maria, think not of your sisters and their matches! They have been fortunate indeed to find such suitable gentlemen, but it was not without cost! But I shall say the very same to you as I did to them." Lady Hayward tilted her head just a fraction, her eyes kind. "You must find a suitable husband for yourself, of course, but he must be a gentleman of *your* choosing. Do not consider a gentleman merely by his title, his wealth or his suitability but rather consider your heart."

Maria frowned.

"My heart?"

"Well," Lady Hayward replied, with a small chuckle,

"there is to be no happiness found in a marriage to a gentleman that one either detests or is very bored by, indeed!"

The sentiment was one that Maria could not help but agree with, although she had to confess herself a little surprised.

"I can understand why you would say such a thing, Lady Hayward."

"That is because I was wed to a gentleman that I cared for very deeply, Lady Maria," came the quiet reply. "And he cared for me also. It was a match which brought with it a good deal of happiness and, if I can do one thing for you, my dear, it will be to find you the very same situation. Do not accept a gentleman's court simply because he is well titled. If you find him dull, disinteresting, arrogant, self-important or entirely ignorant in manners, then there is no need to consider him further!" She smiled and spread her hands. "Do you understand what I mean?"

"I do," Maria replied, softly. "Thank you for your counsel, Lady Hayward."

The lady's smiled broadened and she leaned forward in her seat, jostled just a little by the sway of the carriage.

"Indeed, I have something else to tell you, which I hope will be further reassurance," she continued, as Maria listened intently. "My own daughter, Sophia, is to join us both in London."

A flutter of surprise caught Maria's heart.

"Your daughter?"

"It is to be her first Season, and I do hope that you will be an encouragement to each other," Lady Hayward continued, sounding very happy indeed. "She is a little younger than you, of course, but not by very much. I am hopeful that you will both have an excellent Season."

Maria found her heart lifting from the worries and anxieties that held it, gratified by the thought of having another young lady by her side. Last Season, she had not found anyone in particular to be a close friend or acquaintance and thus, had found herself a little lonely at times. This Season, it seemed, was to be very different indeed.

"I look forward to meeting her," she said, honestly. "When will she arrive?"

Lady Hayward sat back against the squabs, her eyes shining with delight at the thought of seeing her daughter again soon.

"She will arrive with Lord Hayward – her brother – tomorrow afternoon, all being well," she said, sounding quite satisfied. "Hayward himself does not intend to remain in London, however, so he will not be present in the house save for a day or so in order for him to rest before he returns to the estate."

"I see," Maria replied, finding herself a little more excited now that she knew she would soon have a companion. "I do hope that both she and I will have a successful Season."

"I will tell Sophia the very same as I have told to you," Lady Hayward replied, firmly. "Do not think that I expect, or even hope, for my daughter to make a suitable match during her very first Season, Lady Maria. If she enjoys her time here then that is all I hope for her. Truly. Do not think that I shall push you towards making a match either. If it is to be, then it will occur quite naturally and without any particular difficulty."

"And if it is not?" Maria asked, as Lady Hayward smiled.

"Then we shall look to the autumn and winter months, as we did last year," came the swift reply. "Have no doubt, Lady Maria, you will find your match in time. There is no need to worry nor seek to hurry such things along by making hasty decisions or the like." Leaning forward, she pressed Maria's hand for a moment, her gaze steady. "Do not worry. All will be well."

"Might I present my daughter, Lady Sophia."

Maria looked at the young lady for a moment, smiled and then curtsied quickly.

"Good afternoon, Lady Sophia," she said, with as much warmth as she could express. "You must be tired after your journey. Please, do sit down."

Lady Sophia laughed, her blue eyes twinkling.

"I am not at all fatigued, much to my brother's chagrin," she replied, although she did sit down quickly. "Since we left the Inn this morning, I have become more and more eager and my excitement and enthusiasm has, I believe, quite worn Hayward out!"

Lady Hayward chuckled, one hand on her daughter's shoulder for a moment before she reached to ring the bell for tea.

"He does give his apologies and states that he will join us for dinner," Lady Sophia continued, as Maria nodded in understanding. "He is very tired and wishes to rest for a short time so that he will be the very best of company this evening."

"But of course," Maria replied, as Lady Hayward made her way to a vacant chair. She thought Lady Sophia and her mother very similar in appearance, for they both had the same vivid blue eyes and dark hair, although Lady Hayward's was greying. And yet, there was a vivacity about the young lady that Maria knew all too well, given that Lady Hayward expressed the very same in practically everything she did. A sense of contentment and relief washed over her. She was quite certain that, within only a very short time, she and Lady Sophia *would*, in fact, become very good friends indeed.

"I do hope that you will permit me to ask you many questions about London, Lady Maria," Lady Sophia continued, as the door opened for the maids to quickly and quietly bring in trays of refreshment, which were set down before them. "I am very keen to know all I can about how one must act in London, how one can find success!"

Maria allowed herself a small smile, hiding the truth from Lady Sophia. The truth that she herself was not at all certain that she knew how to be successful at all, given that thus far, she had not even been courted by a single gentleman!

"I will do my very best to answer whatever questions you might have," she promised, as Lady Hayward reached to pour tea for them all. "Might I ask, Lady Hayward, if we have received any invitations as yet?"

Lady Hayward chuckled, her eyes twinkling as she glanced up at Maria.

"We have only been in London for a day, Lady Maria," she said, teasingly. "Is there anything – or anyone in particular – you were hoping to meet?"

Maria found herself blushing furiously, despite the fact that there was not a single gentleman whom she considered with any real interest.

"No, indeed not," she said, firmly, although Lady Sophia let out a quiet giggle and hid her mouth with her hand, making Maria's blush deepen. "I just hoped that–"

Lady Hayward handed Maria a cup of tea and then put one hand to her heart.

"I apologize, Lady Maria, for teasing you so," she said, as her daughter lapsed into silence. "Yes, we have received an invitation, in fact." Picking up the second cup and saucer, she set it down in front of Lady Sophia. "We have been invited to our first ball of the Season!" Her eyes were warm as she settled back in her chair, although there was still an apologetic note in her voice. "Lord and Lady Cressington have invited the household, which, I believe, will include you also, Sophia."

At this, Lady Sophia clapped her hands together, her eyes bright with excitement.

"How wonderful!"

"We shall have to make a visit to the modiste's, of course," Lady Hayward continued, as Maria nodded, a swirl of uncertainty now filling her rather than any real excitement. "Your father, Lady Maria, was quite determined that you should have new gowns for this Season, to make certain that they are of the highest fashion."

Maria nodded, albeit a little doubtfully. She was not certain that even the very best of gowns would improve her standing in society. Whatever it was about her last year, she had not exactly made the very best of impressions.

"When should you like to go?" Lady Hayward asked, as Lady Sophia looked towards Maria. "Would tomorrow be too soon, Sophia? I am aware that you have travelled quite a distance and might require a few days' rest."

Lady Sophia laughed and shook her head.

"Mama, I am very excited indeed about being in London and would be inclined to go to the modiste's today, were it not already too late!" she declared, as Maria gave her a small smile, understanding all of the emotions that Lady Sophia was expressing.

She had been the very same last Season, only to find herself sorely disappointed. No offers of courtship, no evident interest from even a single gentleman. It had been the same during the autumn and winter months in London. Was the same going to happen to her this Season? Maria felt her worries begin to mount up, growing to form a great and insurmountable heap in front of her as Lady Hayward and Lady Sophia continued to talk about their intended visit to the dressmaker. She bit her lip, worrying at it for a moment as she thought about the first ball of the Season. Would anyone remember her? Would anyone be glad to see her again, be glad of her company? Would she be asked to dance? Would any gentlemen seek her out for a dance? A faint heat rose in her face as the fear that none present would even *think* to do so began to rise up within her heart.

"Lady Maria?"

She started visibly, lifting her eyes to see Lady Hayward's concerned expression looking back at her.

"Yes?"

"Are you quite all right, my dear?" Lady Hayward asked, that look of concern continuing to grow. "You appear a little distracted."

"I was lost in thought," Maria replied quickly, not wanting to express in detail the truth behind her strange quietness. "I was thinking about the first ball of the Season." A forced smile pulled at her lips but Maria knew that Lady Hayward was not entirely convinced, given the sharp look in her eyes. "I am certain it will be an excellent occasion."

Lady Sophia clapped her hands together, her eyes dancing with evident anticipation.

"I do hope so!" she said, as Lady Hayward continued to study Maria. "You will have to introduce me to all of your acquaintances, Lady Maria."

Maria's heart twisted in her chest as the same fears delved their claws all the deeper.

"But of course," she said, as warmly as she could, despite the fact that Lady Hayward was still watching her with sharp eyes. "I will be very glad to indeed, Lady Sophia." Forcing herself to continue smiling and doing her utmost to set aside her worries in order that she might consider them at a later time, rather than in front of Lady Hayward and her daughter, Maria reached to pick up her teacup and saucer. "Now, did we decide when we are to go to the modiste's?"

Lady Hayward set down her own cup and saucer, finally dropping her gaze from Maria's face.

"We thought the morrow, Lady Maria," she said, as Maria nodded with what she hoped was eagerness. "Should that suit you?"

"It would suit me very well indeed," Maria declared, as Lady Sophia smiled at her warmly. "I look forward to it."

"Our first outing!" Lady Sophia exclaimed, as Maria nodded, smiling indulgently. "Goodness, I do hope that I do not lose my head or behave in a ridiculous fashion!"

"I shall not permit you to do so," Lady Hayward replied, a trifle grimly as her daughter laughed. "But yes, I am sure that tomorrow's foray into London will bring happiness to you both." She smiled at Maria, although there was still a flicker of concern in her gaze. "And then, on to the ball!"

CHAPTER TWO

Making his way into White's, Isaac, Earl of Ridlington sat down heavily in a large, over-stuffed chair which was near the fireplace. He was grati-fied to see that the fire had been lit that evening, pulling some of the spring night's chill from his bones.

"A brandy," he muttered, snapping his fingers at the nearest footman, who nodded and stepped away, leaving Isaac to look steadfastly into the flames of the fire and consider matters carefully.

He had only been in London for a sennight – although, of course, he had been present before many times when it came to matters of business – and already he was finding himself a little overwhelmed. And that was without attending any particular social occasions, although he had, of course, received various invitations. There had been an urge to attend but, given that he had every intention of taking the greatest of care in his acquaintances and in the young ladies he hoped to engage with, Isaac had chosen to remain at home until his thoughts were quite clear.

"Your brandy, my Lord."

Isaac took it from the tray without a word, leaving the footman to step away. He swirled the amber liquid in the glass, sniffing at it appreciatively before taking a small sip. His shoulders dropped just a little as he finally felt himself relax. At least here, he did not have to be so much on his guard.

"Ridlington? Is that you?"

Isaac looked up in surprise, just as a tall, thin gentleman came to stand before him, his sharp eyes searching Isaac's face.

"Good gracious, it *is* you!" the fellow exclaimed, as Isaac did his utmost to recall the gentleman's name. "Do you not recall? We met last year, on a matter of business."

He dropped into a chair and looked across at Isaac with an easy smile playing about his face, just as Isaac – thankfully – managed to recall him.

"Lord Bradstock, is it not?" he asked, as the gentleman's broad grin answered him. "Good evening to you."

"I am very glad that you remember me," came the reply, as Lord Bradstock inclined his head. "Although I must say, I did not expect to see you in London during the Season. Did you not tell me that you only ever came to London when the *beau monde* were gone from it?"

"I did," Isaac replied, with a wave of his hand. "But I have decided that I must find myself a bride and produce the heir that is required of me." He gave a small shrug. "Therefore, I find myself in London."

Lord Bradstock nodded sagely, as though he quite

understood Isaac's reason for returning to London during the Season.

"It can be a little overwhelming at first," he warned, as Isaac took another sip of his brandy. "There are so many young ladies, so many eligible beauties that one does not know quite where to look!"

Isaac chuckled and took another sip of brandy.

"That may be so, but I have very specific requirements as to my bride," he said, as Lord Bradstock's brows rose again. "I am afraid that I will not accept simply any young lady's company."

Lord Bradstock said nothing for a moment, his eyes searching Isaac's only for him to shrug hard.

"Well, it is probably a wise thing for you to be quite certain of what you desire," he replied, as Isaac nodded, satisfied. "That way, you will not waste your time on those who will be entirely unsuitable."

"That is my intention at least," Isaac replied, glad that Lord Bradstock seemed to understand. "Whether or not I can find such a lady amongst the *ton* is quite another thing."

Lord Bradstock opened his mouth to say something, then closed it again before harrumphing, throwing back the rest of his whisky and gesturing for a footman to come near. He ordered another two brandies and then returned his gaze to Isaac.

Isaac said nothing, wondering what it was that Lord Bradstock had been about to say.

"These 'requirements' of yours," Lord Bradstock leant forward in his chair, his elbows on his knees. "Might I be so bold as to ask you what they are?"

For a moment, Isaac hesitated inwardly, not wanting to disclose such private thoughts to a gentleman he barely knew. But, he considered, there was no great embarrassment in any of his requirements and therefore, he should have no need to keep such thoughts to himself.

"Given that my wife will be a Countess, it is obviously important that she is from the very best of families," he began, as Lord Bradstock listened eagerly, nodding fervently as he did so. "I would hope that she would have an excellent dowry and eventual inheritance. It is not that I require any additional funds, but rather that such a thing would show just how suitable a family hers might be."

"I quite understand," Lord Bradstock replied, sitting back just a little. "You would not expect to wed a young lady whose father was a Viscount, then. Or a Baron."

Isaac wrinkled his nose.

"Indeed not," he answered, plainly. "Given that I am an Earl, she must be of equal standing – if not better."

"Of course."

Taking a deep breath and warming to his subject a little more, Isaac continued quickly.

"In addition, I would expect her to have all of the usual and expected accomplishments," he continued, with a wave of his hand. "Good conversation, but with the awareness of when to remain quiet. Playing the pianoforte and perhaps singing also, of course." Tilting his head, Isaac looked away from Lord Bradstock, quickly running through the rest of the things he considered important for any young lady he might consider. "I would be very pleased indeed if she could paint and draw well, hold herself with poise and elegance and, all in all, have an excellence of manner about her."

"You would not wish for an *overly* accomplished wife, then," Lord Bradstock grinned, as Isaac closed his eyes for a moment, his lip curling in distaste. "Nor one that is too quiet and reserved."

"Indeed not!" he exclaimed, very much opposed to the idea already. "Wallflowers and bluestockings will gain none of my attention. The young lady of my choosing must have the confidence to make her way through society with ease but yet know precisely when her conversation is required and when it is best for her to remain silent. She will, in addition, dance very well indeed, be able to write with a fine hand and, all in all, make a more than suitable Countess, should the time come."

Lord Bradstock let out a long breath and sat back in his chair, his eyebrows lifting just a little as he looked back at Isaac. The confidence that Isaac had felt in the beginning, when he had first started to speak, began to wane as he saw the doubt in Lord Bradstock's eyes.

"You think me foolish?"

"No, indeed, I do not!" Lord Bradstock exclaimed, waving one hand about in a determined manner. "No, there is no thought of foolishness in my head, Lord Ridlington. It is only that you have such a great number of requirements that I do wonder if you will be able to find such a creature!"

Isaac said nothing, knowing that he had not spoken of every single consideration which was in his mind, but only the ones which he considered to be of the greatest importance. Nor had he expressed the truth of *why* he spoke with such specificity - but that, he considered, was not worth speaking of. He had come up with the definition of his requirements based solely on what he had witnessed as a child. His father and mother had often been at odds, and the continuous tension and strife had made for a most unpleasant household. When he had been a young man, learning what it meant to be an Earl, his father – a little in his cups – had told him quite plainly that it would be unwise for him to ever marry a lady based solely on a supposed affection. No, he had been told, solemnly, it would be in his best interests to consider carefully the requirements of a wife and to choose his wife that way. The late Lord Ridlington had made it plain that he regretted wedding someone he had simply found himself drawn to and that sentiment had remained with Isaac always.

"It is every gentleman's wish to marry well, of course," Lord Bradstock continued, his eyes now studying Isaac with a sharpness which was a little unsettling. "But it might be somewhat rare to discover a young lady with all of the characteristics that you have stated. I presume, also, that you would hope for her to be something of a beauty?"

Isaac cleared his throat.

"It is not a requirement," he replied, feeling a trifle awkward. "Although I do not think that a plain wife would be of particular advantage." Clearing his throat, he shrugged. "After all, if I am to produce an heir, then she must bear some kind of beauty."

Lord Bradstock chuckled and Isaac managed to smile,

a little relieved that Lord Bradstock had not called such a thought entirely ridiculous.

"In that regard, I am certain that you will not find any of the young ladies of the *ton* to be lacking," he replied, as Isaac nodded indulgently. "There are many fine creatures to be had here in London." He looked back at Isaac for a moment, considering. "And what of those who are newly out this year? Will you consider them?"

Thinking quickly for a moment, Isaac eventually shook his head.

"I do not think I shall, no," he stated, as Lord Bradstock listened with interest. "Young ladies in their first Season are much too flighty, much too ridiculous. They are, from what I have heard, entirely taken up with being in London and overly excited about all that goes on. A young lady who is in her second Season would be quite perfect, however, for she is someone who has already enjoyed her debut and now is ready to seek out a sensible match."

"And what if she is in her third Season?" Lord Bradstock asked, as Isaac's lips twisted. "Will you consider a lady in that particular situation?"

It was on the tip of Isaac's tongue to state that no, he would not, only for him to catch the grin that now pulled at Lord Bradstock's lips. Did the gentleman think him ridiculous?

"I should prefer a lady in her second Season," he answered, eventually. "But a lady in her third Season, I *might* consider, should she fit the rest of my requirements."

That was an acceptable change to make, Isaac

thought to himself, as Lord Bradstock nodded slowly and lifted his brandy glass to his lips. If he could find such a lady then, were she in her third Season, he would consider her regardless. A lady in her third Season, however, tended to suggest that there was something about her that was amiss, something that could not bring the attention of the gentlemen of the *ton* to her.

Lord Bradstock chuckled, shaking his head to himself as he did so. Isaac found himself stiffening, his shoulders lifting just a little as he looked back at the gentleman. Now quite certain that Lord Bradstock found him ridiculous, Isaac did not know what to say or what to do, resisting the urge to throw himself up from his chair and quit White's altogether.

"I do wonder," Lord Bradstock said, still laughing, "whether or not the ladies of the *beau monde* speak of *us* in such a manner?" The embarrassment and mortification that had begun to make its way through Isaac's heart immediately lifted as he realized that the gentleman was not, in fact, mocking him as he had at first thought. "Do you think they would look at us and consider just how many Seasons we had enjoyed before thinking whether or not we would be suitable for them?" Lord Bradstock continued, as Isaac finally began to smile, his hand loosening just a little on his brandy glass. "We do have a great many advantages as gentlemen, do we not?"

Isaac nodded, seeing Lord Bradstock shake his head once more and realizing that what the gentleman said was quite true. He had never once considered whether or not he would be ignored or set aside by a lady of the *ton*, for given that he was an Earl with a substantial fortune, there was everything to recommend him.

"I suspect that the ladies of the *beau monde* have very few requirements when it comes to the gentlemen they consider," he replied, fully aware of the difference between his statement and his own considerations, but finding there to be no particular difficulty there. "But that is simply the way of things." One shoulder lifted in a half-shrug. "I do not expect to have any difficulty in securing the interest of any lady I find to be suitable."

Lord Bradstock lifted his glass in a mock toast. "May you find the greatest success," he replied, as Isaac chuckled. "I suppose that I also should consider the finding myself a bride, as you are doing, but for this Season, I fear that I might very well continue to indulge myself rather than consider it with any real seriousness."

Isaac lifted one eyebrow, studying Lord Bradstock. "Oh?"

"Well," Lord Bradstock replied, with a lop-sided grin, "there is no particular need for me to settle down as yet! I have a younger brother who has done so, *and* produced not one, but two sons already! Should the worst occur, then the title will fall to someone very deserving – and capable, I might add. Quite frankly, I sometimes think that my brother ought to have been the one born first, to have been the one who inherited the title rather than myself, for he certainly would have done much better than I." He looked back steadily at Isaac, his smile fading. "But you have no younger brother, if I recall?"

A little surprised that Lord Bradstock would have remembered such a thing, Isaac nodded.

"I have no family left, save for a few dear old aunts and the like," he said, feeling no sense of sorrow over such a thing. "My mother passed away shortly after I was born and my father some years ago." Taking a mouthful of his brandy, he let the warmth of it spread through his chest before he continued. "The importance of finding a bride has weighed on my heart ever since then, given that I am the only one who can produce the required heir."

"What would happen to your title, should you...?"

Lord Bradstock did not finish his question but Isaac knew what he was asking.

"It would go to a most undeserving cousin," he replied, grimacing. "A distant cousin at that, I might add." He resisted the urge to shudder at the thought of his cousin settling into Ridlington Hall and attempting to shoulder the responsibility which came with the title. He knew him to be a drunkard and a wastrel and feared that, should such a thing ever occur, the title of Ridlington would be forever ruined. "After my father's death, I had to make certain that all matters surrounding the estate were resolved in a satisfactory manner and that the estate itself was proving to be profitable. Now that I have done so, I have set my mind to finding a suitable young lady so that the heir might be produced within the year."

"Very practical," Lord Bradstock agreed, as Isaac settled back in his chair a little more, feeling rather satisfied with himself. "I do hope that all goes as you expect." He tilted his head and looked back at Isaac with a steady gaze. "What have you attended already?"

"Nothing," Isaac replied, aware of the surprise on

Lord Bradstock's face. "But there is a ball tomorrow evening, I believe. Lord and Lady Cressington?"

Lord Bradstock's face cleared.

"Ah yes, that is usually a very enjoyable evening," he said, with the air of someone who had been present at many such occasions. "It is often touted as the most important ball of the Season, given that so many are invited. It is always held at the beginning of the Season also, which will make for a good many introductions to young ladies, I am sure."

Isaac chuckled.

"Then I look forward to attending," he replied, lifting his brandy glass to his lips. "And will you be present also?"

"But of course," Lord Bradstock replied, with a grin. "Given that there are so many eligible young ladies, I could not even *think* of staying away."

A small frown caught Isaac's brow.

"But you said that you have no intention of wedlock?"

Lord Bradstock chuckled.

"Indeed, that is true, but that does not mean that I cannot enjoy the possibilities presented to me! There will be many a conversation to be had, wonderful dances to enjoy and the very best of company." He waggled one finger out towards Isaac. "Mark my words, Lord Ridlington. It will be the very best of evenings."

"Then I look forward to it," Isaac replied, feeling a flurry of anticipation rush through him as Lord Bradstock grinned. "I am sure it will be a very enjoyable evening indeed."

CHAPTER THREE

Maria ran both hands over her skirts as the maid finished dressing her hair. She could not help but feel anxious about this evening, although she had hidden such feelings from both Lady Hayward and Lady Sophia. They had expressed nothing but excitement about the ball whereas Maria herself had begun to feel less and less confident about whether or not she would have any success this Season. This evening's ball was to be the first of their social occasions and, as such, would provide Maria with the answers she required. If she did well, then she would expect her dance card to be filled, her conversations never lacking and acquaintances from both the winter and the previous spring Season recollecting her. To do poorly would be to have her dance card barely touched, to lack conversation and to have no-one showing any particular interest in reacquainting themselves with her.

Maria let out a long slow breath and closed her eyes in an attempt to steady herself. She was desperately beginning to fear that the latter would be what occurred and, in addition, that Lady Sophia would find more success than she.

"You look quite lovely, my Lady."

Maria glanced at her reflection in the mirror and tried to smile, knowing that the maid had done very well. Her long fair hair had been neatly braided and pulled to the top of her head in a loose knot, with a string of pearls around it. A few curls graced her temples, softening her appearance.

"I have put in one or two of your emerald pins, my lady," the maid said, gesturing to the places where she had placed them. Maria turned her head this way and that, seeing the color catch her eye and smiling to herself, aware that the color brought the attention back to her own eyes. They were not as vivid a green as some of her sisters but the emerald pins certainly helped draw attention to them.

"You have done well," she said, as the maid dropped her head and blushed furiously. "Thank you. You need not wait up."

The maid bobbed a curtsy and murmured her thanks, leaving Maria to glance at her reflection once more in the mirror and, satisfied that she looked very well indeed, she made her way from the room.

"Good evening, Lord Cressington."

The gentleman bowed low, his hand holding onto Maria's tightly.

"Good evening, Lady Maria," he replied, his eyes warm as he rose from his bow. "I am very glad to see you again. I do hope that you enjoy the ball this evening."

"I am sure I will," Maria replied with a smile, managing to hide the increasing worry that captured her heart at the sounds of laughter and conversation which came from the ballroom. "Thank you again for your invitation."

She stepped away from Lord and Lady Cressington and waited for Lady Hayward and Lady Sophia to join her. They both took some minutes to converse with their hosts, leaving Maria to stand quietly to one side, looking all around her as she waited.

Lord and Lady Cressington's townhouse was quite lovely, decorated and furnished to the standard expected. Maria allowed her gaze to rove all around her, only to settle on a gentleman who was, as she was doing, standing quietly to one side, his head lowered as he studied something in his hand.

Maria did not know what it was about him that drew her attention, particularly since she was not acquainted with him but, as she watched, she felt her curiosity grow. Most gentlemen, once they had greeted the hosts, would hurry into the ballroom in eager anticipation, whereas this gentleman seemed to be quite contented to linger in the hallway. Was he waiting for someone? What was it that he held in his hand? It could not be the invitation, since that would have already been handed to the footman upon arrival. Maria tilted her head just a fraction, wondering if there was something wrong. Was he concerned about some matter or other? Had he any intention of stepping into the ballroom at all, or would he turn on his heel and then quickly depart?

It was just as she thought this that the gentleman in question looked up and, unfortunately for Maria, directly at her so that their eyes met. Immediately, Maria's dropped her gaze, her cheeks flushing with embarrassment at having been caught staring at him in such a ridiculous fashion.

"Lady Maria?" She looked up, seeing Lady Hayward's quizzical look. "I apologize for making you wait for us," Lady Hayward continued, as Maria forced herself not to look again at the gentleman, despite a strange urge to do so, as though she wanted to see if he was continuing to look at her. "Lady Cressington wanted to ask Sophia many questions!"

"Which I was all too glad to answer," Lady Sophia added, with a smile. "Now..." She turned towards the ballroom door where two footmen stood, ready to open the doors for them so that they might enter. "Are we to step inside?"

Lady Hayward laughed and took Maria's arm, falling into step alongside her daughter.

"Do not lose your head, Sophia," she said, a note of teasing warning in her voice. "You must do all you can to behave with absolute propriety and gentility, as Lady Maria does. Regard her. Emulate her. And I am sure that all will be well."

Maria managed to smile, but felt none of the eagerness which was expressed on Lady Sophia's face. She did not want Lady Sophia to watch her in the way that Lady Hayward had suggested, not when she carried so many worries within her. But then, the doors to the ballroom opened and she was swept inside, her breath hitching as the crashing sounds of conversation, laughter and music all flung themselves at her at once. It was almost as though she had never left, as though she had always been in London. The last few months at home faded away to nothing as she looked all about her, seeing the swirling colors of the gowns and the vividness of the attire of the somewhat foppish gentlemen. There was so much to take in, and yet she could not simply stand there and look all about her until she felt more prepared! Instead, she was borne along with Lady Hayward and Lady Sophia, who was already exclaiming loudly about all that she could see.

"Lady Hayward! Lady Maria!"

Maria's heart leapt in her chest, a swell of relief rushing through her as she greeted a lady she knew to be Lady Whitford. Her mind scrambled to recall the name of Lady Whitford's daughter, however, although she did not see the young lady anywhere nearby.

"How very good to see you again, Lady Whitford," Lady Hayward said, as they rose from their curtsy. "You recall Lady Maria, of course, and might I also present my daughter, Lady Sophia?"

Lady Whitford's eyes flared for a moment, although her smile remained just as beaming and just as joyous as before.

"How wonderful to meet you!" she exclaimed, practically exuberant in her greeting and startling Maria somewhat. "You will have to be introduced to my daughter, Miss Blake, although – as you may have guessed given my state of delight – she is soon to be Lady Moffat!"

Maria murmured her congratulations, trying to find it in her heart to be delighted and pleased for Miss Blake, but inwardly finding herself rather sorrowful indeed. If she recalled correctly, Miss Blake had been a very quiet creature. In fact, Maria had heard her described as a wall-flower on occasion – and now, here she was finding herself engaged to Viscount Moffat? Maria was glad indeed that the young lady had found such happiness but it simply made her question all the more why she herself had not been successful. To have not even a single offer of courtship was, Maria considered, a little embarrassing.

"Lady Maria?"

She turned, leaving Lady Hayward and Lady Whit-ford to continue to converse, a smile leaping into her features as she saw Lord Milson bowing low.

"Good evening, Lord Milson," she said quickly, as the gentleman rose. "You have returned to London, I see."

She smiled warmly, although she knew in her heart that the gentleman before her did not arouse any partic-ular interest within her heart. She was grateful to see him, however, hoping desperately that he might wish to sign her dance card.

"I have, Lady Maria," he replied, with a small smile. "I look forward to your considerations on the shipping disputes between our great nation and the Americas, Lady Maria, which I am certain you already have an opinion on."

Lady Sophia, who had been standing quietly until this moment, then chose to speak.

"Shipping disputes?" she asked, as Maria felt a faint rush of heat begin to climb up into her face.

"Oh, I do apologize for my unladylike interest in such a topic," said Maria. She curtsied quickly, clearly realizing just how foolish she had been. "I ought not to have spoken so. Do forgive me."

Maria gestured to Lady Sophia dully, realizing now that Lord Milson had been speaking with irony and derision, which he had hidden behind his words very well indeed.

"Might I present Lady Sophia, daughter to Lady Hayward, with whom you are already acquainted," she said, as Lady Sophia dropped into a curtsey. "And Lady Sophia, this is the Earl of Milson."

Lord Milson bowed low, a charming smile placed upon his lips as he looked at Lady Sophia.

"How wonderful to make your acquaintance, Lady Sophia," he said, without so much as glancing at Maria. "You may now ask me as many questions as you wish about the shipping disputes, for I am entirely at your service."

Lady Sophia giggled, her eyes bright as she glanced from Lord Milson to Maria and back again.

"I should not have pried, Lord Milson," she replied, a smile still spreading across her face. "Although I confess that I am not that well acquainted with Lady Maria as yet, though I am certain we shall be very soon."

Lord Milson's brows rose and he inclined his head in a most genteel fashion.

"Then permit me to enlighten you, if I may?" he asked, looking at Maria with wide eyes as though he was seeking her permission. "I was introduced to Lady Maria last Season and would be glad to tell you what I know of her."

Maria swallowed hard, feeling a tightness in her throat and trying her best to keep her composure. Lord Milson was not a cruel gentleman but he had, on occasion, made a sharp remark in company about her particular thoughts or opinions. She had not thought him unkind but now she began to wonder if that consideration was not a true representation of his character.

"Please, I should be very glad to hear the many kind things I am sure that you have to say about Lady Maria," Lady Sophia replied eagerly, clearly thinking that Lord Milson would be nothing but generous in his remarks. "She is, from what I know thus far, a very considerate and thoughtful young lady."

Lord Milson laughed quietly, his eyes glinting.

"To state that Lady Maria is very thoughtful is a very accurate description, Lady Sophia," he said, as Maria tried to force a smile to her lips in order to keep the situation as pleasant as she could. "Lady Maria is a very well-read young lady, and has clearly thought about many a matter. In fact, she has no qualms about sharing her opinions with anyone who might be interested!"

Maria flushed and looked away, hearing the note of derision in Lord Milson's voice and finding herself both embarrassed and irritated. Lord Milson had no need to speak of her in such a fashion and was doing so either to torment her for his own pleasure, or simply because he thought it best for Lady Sophia to know of her inclination to share what she thought on various matters. Maria was not ashamed of doing such a thing, for she had always prided herself on being fully aware of matters of importance. She was not inclined towards painting or drawing, singing or the pianoforte. Rather, she wished only to read and to read well so that she might improve her mind. Her father had not prevented it, Lady Hayward had made no mention of it being an issue, and Maria had never once considered such a thing to be either embarrassing or unwelcome.

Not until this moment.

"It is an excellent thing to be so well-informed, I think." Maria looked at Lady Sophia, a little surprised to hear the hardness in her voice. "I should like to know more of the world and all that goes on within it – such as the disputes you speak of, Lord Milson," Lady Sophia continued. "How wonderful it must be to be able to talk of such things with a full and accurate awareness rather than having no knowledge whatsoever!"

A small, tentative smile crept across Maria's face as she looked at Lady Sophia, seeing the way the smile had gone completely from her face as she gazed at Lord Milson. One glance towards Lord Milson told Maria that he was not at all pleased with Lady Sophia's response, having expected quite the opposite.

"Well," he muttered, covering up his misstep with nothing more than a quick smile and a clearing of his throat. "Indeed. That is to say..." He threw a look towards Maria who simply arched one eyebrow, making him shuffle his feet with evident awkwardness. "A dance, Lady Sophia?" His voice was loud and rather nonchalant, as though the previous conversation had not even occurred. "If you would be so willing, that is?"

Lady Sophia looked towards Maria, who merely lifted one shoulder to indicate that it was entirely Lady Sophia's decision. She did not mind that Lord Milson had not asked *her* to dance, for she was not at all inclined towards him. Instead, she watched as Lady Sophia eventually nodded and slipped her dance card from her wrist before handing it to Lord Milson.

He wrote his name hurriedly and then, with a sharp bow, excused himself from their company, disappearing into the crowd with the greatest of speed.

"Well!" Lady Sophia declared, the moment he had stepped away from them. "I declare, Lady Maria, I have never met a gentleman with such a rude manner! I cannot believe that he spoke of you in that sort of condescending tone!"

Maria let out a small sigh, grateful for Lady Sophia's support and clear upset on her behalf, but still feeling a little awkward about the entire encounter.

"There are gentlemen such as Lord Milson throughout society, Lady Sophia," she answered, quietly. "Pray, take no notice of him. I was acquainted with him last Season and did not think poorly of him then." She spread her hands. "It seems that this Season, he is a little more... sharply spoken."

Lady Sophia shook her head and tutted.

"I should have refused to dance with him," she stated, as Maria laughed softly. "He does not deserve my company."

"Indeed, he does not," Maria agreed, determinedly.

"But you should not refuse to stand up with him now that you gave him your card." She laughed again, feeling the tension dissipate completely and a new sense of companionship beginning to grow between them. "But I am sure that you will find many more favorable gentlemen to dance with."

"As I hope you do also," Lady Sophia replied, fervently. "For Lord Milson is not at *all* what I would consider a gentleman. I shall be glad to end our acquaintance the moment I step from the dance floor!" She looked at Maria for a long moment, now appearing rather thoughtful. "Might I ask you something?"

Maria nodded.

"But of course."

"When he spoke of these 'shipping disputes' – whatever they are – might I ask if you were already aware of them? You understood what he spoke of?"

Hesitating for a moment, Maria looked back at Lady Sophia and chose to speak honestly.

"I do understand," she replied, softly. "I have read about them recently and, if I were honest, I do have an opinion on the matter."

She winced inwardly as Lady Sophia's eyes widened, clearly rather astonished that Maria should know about these things which were, more often than not, reserved for only the gentlemen's conversations. Maria knew very well that she was a little unusual in terms of her interest in such things, but Lady Hayward had not discouraged her from it and thus, she had been quite open about her opinions and considerations, no matter who she had been speaking to. Yes, there had been a few astonished looks, and one or two murmurs of surprise, but that had never prevented her from continuing, in any way. A sudden flare of doubt rose in her chest. Was this why she had not achieved any success these last two visits to London? Was her outspoken manner, her appearance of knowing more than perhaps was deemed right, dissuading gentlemen from considering her? She did not want to believe it, did not even want to *think* of it but, at that very moment, she felt a very heavy burden settle over her shoulders. Perhaps this was all her own doing, and it had not been until this moment that she had realized it.

"Lady Maria, might I ask you something?"

She was pulled back to their conversation, seeing what appeared to be embarrassment flood Lady Sophia's face as she nodded. Lady Sophia's cheeks were a little flushed and she looked away for a moment, mayhap considering what words she wished to use, so that she would not upset Maria in any way. Maria wondered if Lady Sophia was about to ask her the very same thing that she had just asked herself – whether or not this knowledge had, in any way, assisted in, or detracted from, her search for a suitable match – and she would have to be honest with her answer.

"Might you help me, Lady Maria?"

Maria frowned, glancing behind them as Lady Hayward laughed at something her friend had said.

"Help you?" she asked, looking back at Lady Sophia in confusion. "I do not know what you mean. What can I do that your mother cannot?"

Lady Sophia's brows knotted together and she spread her hands wide.

"I feel so very foolish, Lady Maria," she said, speaking with such honesty that Maria was a little taken aback. "I have never been to London before and, whilst my mother has, and will guide me very well, in the way that she has led your elder sisters to suitable matches, I cannot help but feel that I am somewhat lacking."

"I do not understand," Maria replied, feeling all the more confused. "There is nothing about you that is lacking, Lady Sophia."

"Oh, but there is!" she said, earnestly, taking a small step closer to Maria. "I may well have the usual accomplishments, but I lack the experience of conversing with those around me. I find myself overwhelmed and behaving a little foolishly – as you yourself witnessed when I spoke without thinking to Lord Milson." Her lips twisted and she shook her head, her eyes dropping to the floor for a moment. "Even though I was not out, my brother permitted me to attend one or two small social gatherings near to our estate, and there, I found myself doing the very same as I have done this evening! I need your guidance, Lady Maria. You must tell me when I am making a dreadful mistake and explain to me what I must do instead."

Maria hesitated, not quite certain that she could do what Lady Sophia was asking of her and yet rather reluctant to refuse, given the young lady's earnestness.

"Pray do not refuse!" Lady Sophia exclaimed, evidently seeing the doubt in Maria's expression. "This evening, for example, I am not at all certain what I am meant to speak of during my dance with Lord Milson! What if I speak poorly, or without careful thought, and then news of my foolishness goes through all of the *ton*? What shall I do then? I am so very eager to make a good impression."

"When it comes to Lord Milson, I think you would be wise not to say anything at all!" Maria replied, a ghost of a smile on her lips. "Very well, Lady Sophia, although I confess I do not think that I shall be of very much aid to you at all."

Lady Sophia's shoulders slumped with relief, and her eyes were wide as one hand reached out to catch Maria's wrist.

"Oh, thank you!" she exclaimed, as Maria tried to smile but felt no confidence within her heart. "I am sure you shall be a great help to me, Lady Maria. You clearly are very well aware of what I ought to be speaking of, for example and –"

"In that, I shall set you to rights," Maria interrupted. "I have only just considered that mayhap my opinions and considerations on certain matters are what pushes various gentlemen from my company. It might very well be why they do not consider me for courtship." One shoulder lifted in a half shrug as a frown returned to Lady Sophia's face. "I am, I will admit, a bluestocking and, thus far, have not attempted to hide my interest in matters of business, politics or philosophy. However, it may be that I should hide such things from the *beau monde*, for fear that they think poorly of me because of it." She shook her head and sighed, feeling a slight kick of guilt at the idea of hiding a true part of herself from any potential suitor, although, she considered, if she *was* to be courted by any one gentleman, she would then have opportunity to reveal such a thing to him, if it was required. "I should pretend to be just as every other young lady of the *ton*, I think. I can still speak well, but without making it apparent just how much I might know about a subject. Although I do not think that I can hide my lack of talent on the pianoforte, or my abysmal attempts at painting!"

Lady Sophia giggled, her eyes dancing.

"Then you shall pretend that some of my paintings are yours!" she replied, as Maria laughed, her heavy burden lessened just a little by Lady Sophia's blithe manner. "And should anyone wish to hear you play the pianoforte, I shall sit by you and pretend to turn the pages or some such thing, so that they are entirely convinced you are quite the musician!"

"You are very kind," Maria replied, still smiling. "Mayhap I shall have to do so at some point, if I am ever blessed enough to have a gentleman consider calling upon me!" She tilted her head and looked back at Lady Sophia, realizing suddenly that they might be able to assist each other in such matters. "Perhaps, Lady Sophia, in doing what you have suggested, you may be of help to me also, in the way that you hope I shall be a help to you. I must shed my true self, it seems, and pretend to be the accomplished young lady that the *ton* expects. I must think of nothing but fashion plates and the like, making certain to go to the milliners before the bookshop."

"I very much enjoy studying the fashion plates, I confess," Lady Sophia replied, sounding a little doubtful.

"Excellent!" Maria replied, now a little more eager in her considerations. "Then you will instruct me as to what is the very height of fashion at the moment, tell me how to speak of them and the like, and I shall do very well indeed, I am sure."

Lady Sophia hesitated, no smile lingering in her expression. She studied Maria for some moments, giving an air of uncertainty that Maria did not quite understand. She herself felt quite determined to throw aside her true self and, instead, take on a façade which was entirely what the *ton* expected. Mayhap then she would finally be able to secure a suitable gentleman and would not have to endure returning home without even the smallest hint of success. Her father was patient, yes, but she did not want to be the spinster of the family, who, no matter how hard she tried, never achieved the happy situation of marriage.

"It would be something of a falsehood, would it not?"

Maria considered Lady Sophia's question and then nodded, ignoring the warning that rang in her ears.

"It would be, yes," she agreed, quietly. "But I confess, Lady Sophia, I have not had any gentleman displaying even a single iota of interest in me during last Season nor during the autumn and winter months. Therefore, I will do whatever I can to change that particular situation."

"And if a gentleman *should* court you?" Lady Sophia asked, her eyes still worried. "What then? Will you tell him the truth of yourself?"

"I shall find a way to do so," Maria answered, waving the question away and telling herself that she need not consider it at present. "But I am sure that all will be quite well, Lady Sophia. We will both be an aid to each other and, in doing so, might very well each find our own individual happiness."

Lady Sophia hesitated and then shrugged.

"Very well," she said, quietly. "Although I should inform you, Lady Maria, that I fully intend to find a gentleman who is not only suitable, but brings an affection to my heart."

Maria was a little surprised by such a remark, only to remember that such a sentiment had also been expressed by Lady Hayward. She considered it for a moment and then nodded.

"I think that would be the very best of situations, certainly," she agreed, slowly. "I admire you very much for being so determined, Lady Sophia."

"You do not seek such a gentleman?" Lady Sophia asked, a little more gently. "You are contented with suitability only?"

Again, Maria hesitated, not quite knowing how to answer. She had never been of a particular opinion, having hoped and, indeed, expected that gentlemen would come to seek her out and that she might, therefore, have a choice of who to consider.

"I shall think on it," she replied, as Lady Sophia smiled, clearly glad to hear Maria's response. "Well, Lady Sophia, it seems that we are to become very dear friends indeed!"

"I am very glad to hear it!" came the voice of Lady Hayward, making both Maria and Lady Sophia jump in surprise. "Goodness, I did not mean to startle you both!" Lady Hayward continued, laughing. "You must have been very deep in conversation."

"We were indeed," Maria replied, although she knew by the tiny shake of Lady Sophia's head not to mention a word of what had been discussed between them – not that she herself had any intention of doing so. "Lord Milson has written his name upon Lady Sophia's dance card, Lady Hayward, and I was just advising her on his... demeanor."

"Oh." Lady Hayward looked towards her daughter, who smiled but said nothing. "I am very grateful to you, Lady Maria. It would be best for Sophia to know which gentlemen to give little thought to, so that she does not give her time nor her consideration to them." Smiling a little more brightly and settling her shoulders, Lady Hayward seemed to catch someone else's attention, looking past Maria's as she did so. "And now it seems that Lord Bradstock is to reacquaint himself with you, Lady Maria. See, if you turn now, he is coming directly towards you."

Maria's heart did not leap with delight nor her stomach tighten with anticipation as she did so, making sure to greet Lord Bradstock warmly. Lord Bradstock was certainly a charming gentleman, but was not at all inclined towards courtship, or even giving matrimony the smallest of considerations. He would be a pleasant dance partner, certainly and that, at least, would remove some of her shame this evening. She would not be without at least one dance and that, certainly, was a very great relief indeed.

CHAPTER FOUR

I saac watched as Lord Bradstock led yet another young lady out onto the dance floor. He considered what he felt, aware of some great emotion that tugged at his heart, but not yet fully certain of what it was. *Jealousy?* He shook his head and allowed himself a quiet laugh. He was not at all jealous of Bradstock, who made his way with ease through the crowd, but yet had no true consideration for his own situation at present. No, he was not jealous. Surely. He could not have any envy for Bradstock's ease of manner, for the way that the ladies of the *beau monde* seemed simply to flock to him.

Wincing inwardly, Isaac realized that the very thing he was trying to deny was precisely what he felt. There *was* a jealousy there. There went Bradstock into the crowd of guests, writing his name on seemingly endless dance cards and, thereafter, accompanying a different lady out onto the floor for each set, whereas he stood, silent and alone, in the corner of the ballroom. He was not yet well acquainted with any particular persons, although there were a few gentlemen that he knew, but there was certainly within him a lack of confidence that prevented him from simply seeking out an introduction one way or the other.

"Foolish man."

He muttered to himself, as his eyes roved over the crowd of guests rather aimlessly, looking from one person to the next, doing his utmost to find someone else that he recognized. He would have to step out from the shadows soon and make his way a little more into the ballroom if he ever wanted to be introduced to some of the young ladies of the *ton*.

His gaze suddenly caught on one particular young lady, who was speaking earnestly to another. He recognized her as the young lady who had been standing in the hallway earlier that evening, the one who had been watching him with evidently great curiosity. It had been something of an embarrassment, Isaac had to admit, for he had been standing to one side of the hallway in an attempt to push aside his anxiety about stepping out into the ballroom, whilst pretending to do something different altogether. When he had looked up, he had caught her gaze for only a moment, but it had been enough for him to know her face. She was fair haired, with big, bright eyes that continually seemed to catch his attention. There was a certain softness to her expression, particularly when she smiled, and Isaac found himself considering whether or not she would be someone of interest to him.

"And that is foolishness itself!" he exclaimed, looking away from the lady and berating himself a little more.

"You have seen the lady once and already you are considering –"

He stopped dead, flushing with embarrassment as he realized that one or two other guests had overheard him speaking to himself. Knowing that he could not remain where he stood, Isaac cleared his throat, set his shoulders and stepped out.

He did not know where he was going, nor who he might speak to, and thus made his way somewhat aimlessly through the crowd.

"Lord Ridlington!"

Looking over his shoulder, Isaac let out a silent breath of relief as Lord Bradstock beckoned him near. As much as he did not like to admit that there was a certain jealousy in his heart over Bradstock's ease of manner with those of the *ton*, Isaac knew that Bradstock was more than willing to aid him in introductions and the like. He himself had been too ashamed to ask for his aid directly, however.

"Good evening, Lord Bradstock."

"Good evening!" Bradstock grinned, gesturing to the young lady before him, who now stood with someone Isaac presumed was her mother. "My dear Lady Forester, might I be permitted to present the Earl of Ridlington? He has not been to London for the Season before... much like you, Miss Fawkes."

The young lady blushed furiously and Isaac threw a sharp glance towards Bradstock before he bowed and murmured a greeting to both of the ladies in turn. Surely Bradstock recalled that Isaac had no interest in young women in their first Season? Bradstock looked back at him directly as Isaac rose and gave him a small shrug, a smile playing about his mouth.

"I know that Lord Ridlington is eager to make many new acquaintances," he continued, airily. "I am doing all I can to make certain that he becomes very well known amongst the *beau monde*, for we must make him feel welcome, must we not?"

"Oh, indeed we must!" Lady Forester exclaimed, her expression filled with delight. "I am very glad to meet you, Lord Ridlington."

"Ah." Bradstock settled a hand on Isaac's arm. "I can now see *another* of my acquaintances that I must greet this evening. She is just over there." He pointed vaguely to his right. "Do come and join me once you have finished conversing. I will be glad to introduce you to another few friends."

Isaac did not have time to protest, nor to remind Bradstock of the specific requirements of the young ladies he sought introduction to, for his friend stepped away almost at once, leaving Isaac to converse with Lady Forester and her doe-eyed daughter.

"Your dance card, Miss Fawkes?" he found himself asking, despite lacking all desire to do so. "I do hope it is not yet full. I have been a little tardy this evening and have not yet sought out any young ladies to dance with. Might I hope that I will find myself able to step out with you?"

The words came to his lips easily enough, but he detested the bright, flickering shard of hope which came into the young lady's eyes as she laughed and handed him the dance card. He had no intention, of course, of seeking out Miss Fawkes again, for she was quite young and awed by London society, and he did not want to even *consider* such a creature. Yes, she might very well be eligible, be beautiful and have an excellent family situation, but if she was only in her first Season, then Isaac could not consider her. The dance card signed, he conversed for a few minutes more and then made his way to where Bradstock stood, leaving a seemingly elated Miss Fawkes behind. He could only pray that he would not put a foot wrong during their quadrille together, for that would be a very great embarrassment indeed!

"I am quite certain that it will not be so," he heard Bradstock say, as Isaac drew near, clearing his throat gently as he did so. He could not see the ladies whom Bradstock spoke to as yet, but Bradstock quickly glanced towards him and then turned to welcome him into their conversation.

"Lord Ridlington!" Bradstock exclaimed in that same, easy manner that Isaac had come to expect. "Wonderful. You have just come from Miss Fawkes and Lady Forester, yes?"

Isaac nodded, looking towards the first young lady who was, by now, blushing just a little – although he was quite certain that it came from nothing that he had done, but instead, from whatever Bradstock had said.

"Wonderful!" Bradstock exclaimed. "Then permit me, if I may, to introduce you? Ladies, this is the Earl of Ridlington, who has only just come to London for the Season." He smiled and gestured to the lady who stood in the middle of the small group. "Might I present Lady Hayward? And this is her daughter, Lady Sophia. And lastly, Lady Maria, who is daughter to the Duke of Landon."

"He is not present this evening," the young lady said, as she dropped into a curtsy. "I reside with Lady Hayward for the Season." She looked up at him and smiled, only for her smile to become a little fractured as a rush of crimson seared her cheeks. "How – how good to meet you, Lord Ridlington."

Isaac stared back at her for a moment, recognizing her to be the young lady whom he had caught watching him in the hallway and who, herself, had then caught his attention earlier that evening. Realizing that he had said nothing in some moments and that both Lady Hayward and Lady Sophia were now waiting for him to speak, Isaac cleared his throat gruffly and placed his hands behind his back.

"I am very glad to make your acquaintance," he said, honestly, dragging his eyes away from Lady Maria. "As Lord Bradstock has said, this is my first foray into London society during the Season, so I am not particularly well acquainted with many of the guests at present. Lord Bradstock is determined to introduce me to practically everyone in London, it seems, for which I am very grateful."

He shot a glance towards Bradstock, who was grinning at this remark, mayhap aware of the odd look between Isaac and Lady Maria.

"I am sure that you will be made very welcome," Lady Hayward said, as Isaac kept his gaze far from Lady Maria. "It is my daughter's first year in London also and thus far, we have found everyone very kind indeed."

She glanced towards her daughter who, after a moment, nodded fervently although she said nothing.

"I am sure I shall, Lady Hayward," Isaac replied, only to recall that he ought now to ask for the two young ladies' dance cards so that he might sign his name for one of their dances. A strange reluctance rose up within him as he turned to Lady Maria, finding himself less than inclined to dance with her given just how awkward things were between them at present. He would much prefer simply to acquaint himself with her and then move away rather than further his acquaintance in any way but, given what was now expected of him, Isaac knew he could not.

"Might I enquire as to whether you would wish to dance this evening, Lady Maria?" he said, before turning to Lady Sophia. "You also, Lady Sophia?"

"Goodness, we are very favored this evening!" Lady Sophia replied, her eyes twinkling as she looked to Lady Maria. "First Lord Bradstock seeks a dance from us and now you also, Lord Ridlington!" She presented him her dance card with a flourish. "I should be very glad to dance, thank you."

Isaac took it from her and then turned to Lady Maria, looking at her expectantly. A slow flush was rising up her neck and into her face as she caught his gaze for a moment, only to drop her head and pull her dance card from her wrist.

"How very generous," she murmured, as he took it from her. "Thank you, Lord Ridlington."

Still feeling that sense of awkwardness between them – and silently wondering if Lady Hayward or Bradstock were aware of it also — Isaac quickly set himself to the task of writing his name down on both of the dance cards. He chose the cotillion for Lady Sophia and the country dance for Lady Maria, deciding, quite certainly, that he would do no more than those three dances this evening. That was more than enough for him at present.

"The cotillion, Lady Sophia," he said, handing it back to her and seeing the dazzling smile she gave him. "And the country dance, Lady Maria."

Lady Maria took the dance card from him and murmured her thanks, although her gaze did not quite rest on him as she did so. Isaac smiled as warmly as he could and turned back to Lady Hayward.

"I should ask you to dance also, Lady Hayward, but I can see that you are already quite caught up with your duties," he said, as Lady Hayward smiled back at him. "Otherwise, of course, I should have asked you also."

"You are very kind, Lord Ridlington," came the reply. "I am sure that my daughter and Lady Maria will be the very best of partners, however, when the time comes."

"I am glad to hear it," he replied, before bowing low and, after a few more minutes of stilted conversation, finally managing to take his leave.

"It is time for the country dance, I believe."

Isaac winced and looked away.

"Then I must go in search of Lady Maria," he said, a little frustrated.

"Whatever is the matter with Lady Maria?" Bradstock asked, as he turned his head to look back sharply at Isaac. "I noticed that there was a tension between you whenever you spoke. Have you already been acquainted?"

Isaac shook his head.

"No, indeed not," he said, briefly explaining what had occurred. "I should very much like to know why she was staring at me so."

Bradstock threw back his head and let out a loud guffaw, which drew the attention of some of the other guests around them and caused Isaac to grimace with embarrassment.

"My dear Ridlington, I am afraid that you will have to become used to one or two young ladies looking at you in such a manner!" Bradstock explained, still laughing. "You are titled, wealthy and I am quite certain that they think you handsome. What does it matter if Lady Maria was watching you so? It may be that she thinks of you in such terms."

This did not make Isaac's thoughts settle into any sort of calm or collected manner for he shook his head sharply and tried to ignore Bradstock's laughter. He could not explain to his friend that there was something about Lady Maria which had drawn his attention also, could not quite make plain that the way he had looked at her had made something within him shift, something that, as yet, he could not understand.

"Go and dance with the lady and allow this tension to dissipate," Bradstock finished, wiping his eyes with his hand as though what Isaac had said had brought him so much mirth, he could not contain it. "She is a very lovely creature and might, in fact, be someone for you to consider."

His eyebrows waggled in a most uncouth manner and Isaac let out a muttered exclamation before he stepped away, knowing that he could not be rude and simply allow the dance to go past without going in search of Lady Maria. It did not take long to find her and, much to Isaac's frustration, his breath seemed to catch in his chest as her eyes caught his. Whatever was this strange reaction to her? He could not explain it and yet it was very unsettling indeed. He had never once considered the fact that he might find himself drawn to a particular young lady when it came to his requirements for a wife. Of course, if Lady Maria did not meet such requirements in any way, then he could not allow himself to consider her further and, if he were honest with himself, Isaac was not certain he even *wished* for such a thing. It would be very strange indeed to have any sort of emotions as regarded his wife, surely? He wanted nothing but practicality and the like, and had never once considered the fact that he might come to care for his bride.

"Lady Maria." He bowed low, aware of the gruffness in his voice. "I believe it is the country dance."

When he raised his head, he saw her bobbing a quick curtsey, her eyes not quite managing to meet his.

"But of course," she said, as Lady Hayward nodded warmly, gesturing for Lady Maria to make her way out towards him. "Thank you, Lord Ridlington."

When she settled her hand on his arm, Isaac felt such a rush of heat climb up through it and into his chest that, for a moment, he stood stock still, staring down at her in disbelief. It was only when her eyes finally met his that he forced himself to step forward, trying to push away such a feeling so that he might focus entirely on the dance instead.

"Do you enjoy dancing, Lady Maria?"

It was an awkward question but, in the silence that had wrapped itself around them, Isaac had struggled to know what to say. He glanced down at the lady as they made their way to the floor, seeing the color in her face.

"I do," came the quiet reply. She looked back up at him, her eyes searching his for a moment rather than pulling her gaze away again in an instant. "Lord Ridlington, I must apologize."

They were on the floor now and he stepped back from her, finding his place and she finding hers.

"Oh?"

"I – I should apologize for staring at you earlier this evening," she replied, her face flaming with embarrassment but her voice remaining quite steady. "It was most improper of me and I cannot apologize enough."

Isaac cleared his throat, his hands behind his back as the music began.

"I see."

"I merely wondered what it was that held you back from the ballroom," she continued, as the music began, making her sink into another curtsey as he bowed low. "But it was rude of me to be so curious and I cannot imagine what you must have thought."

Beginning the dance, Isaac was forced to wait a few moments before he could speak to her again, their steps not taking them together immediately. He let her words sink into his heart, finding himself a little relieved that she had spoken of what had occurred rather than letting it fester into yet a deeper tension that surely would have set them both asunder for the remainder of the Season. He felt the tension slowly leave his body as he looked back at her, finding himself both grateful and relieved that she had spoken so.

"Let us set the matter aside entirely, Lady Maria," he said, as they finally came together in the dance. "I am sure I must have appeared a very curious figure indeed, to be standing in such a manner!" He gave her the ghost of a smile which she acknowledged with one of her own. "I was... waiting for a friend to arrive," he lied, not wanting to express the truth of his reasons for being so tardy. "That is all."

"I see." She turned her head away as the steps bore her away from him, leaving him to wait for yet another few moments before she came near to him again. "I am grateful to you for your understanding, Lord Ridlington."

"But of course," he replied, feeling as though a great weight had shifted from his shoulders. "Let us speak no more about it, Lady Maria."

Her eyes lifted once more to his and, this time, he saw a spark of happiness in her gaze that had not been present before.

"What then shall we speak of, Lord Ridlington?" she asked, a teasing note in her voice. "Now that we are not to discuss the awkward situation that first befell us, what shall we talk about for the remainder of the dance?"

Isaac laughed and looked away from her reluctantly

as he continued the dance, knowing it would not be long before he was back with her again.

"I do not know, Lady Maria," he replied, as they drew near to each other again. "Should we discuss politics? The current state of the British empire?"

He meant this as nothing more than gentle teasing, having no real expectations that she would be able to discuss such matters at all but, for whatever reason, the smile instantly dropped from Lady Maria's face and she did not laugh along with him as he chuckled.

"I hardly think I should know of such things as that, Lord Ridlington," she replied, a little more tightly than before. "You will have to forgive me."

Feeling as though he had made some sort of misstep, Isaac tried to smile at her and was all the more relieved when the dance came to an end. "Forgive me if I have offended you, Lady Maria," he begged, bowing towards her as she curtsied. "I meant nothing by it."

"No, I am sure you did not," she answered, accepting his arm without hesitation as they turned to make their way from the dance floor. "The truth is, Lord Ridlington, that unless you wish to discuss what my opinion is on the various gowns that I can see this evening, or perhaps the latest piece of gossip I have heard, my conversation will be quite useless!"

"Not at all," he reassured her, as they drew near to Lady Hayward. "You shall find me quite eager to talk with you again, Lady Maria. I can assure you of that."

Her eyes met his and, for a moment, she simply stood and looked back at him, studying him carefully. And then, she smiled warmly and removed her hand from his arm.

"Thank you, Lord Ridlington," she replied, although quite what she was thanking him for, Isaac did not know. "That was very pleasant indeed."

"I am glad," he replied, realizing now that their conversation and time together was at an end. "Do enjoy the rest of the evening, Lady Maria."

"I shall," she answered, before, finally, Isaac stepped away and left her in the care of Lady Hayward once more.

CHAPTER FIVE

M aria winced as she sat down at the pianoforte, making Lady Sophia laugh.

"You cannot surely be as bad as you say," she replied, with a shake of her head. "I shall not believe it."

Maria settled her hands on the keys and felt her heart begin to beat a little faster. Her younger sister, Dorothea, played very well indeed and her performances had always left Maria feeling more than a little inadequate.

"Truly I am a very poor player indeed," Maria told Lady Sophia, who continued to look less than convinced. "I have never studied it at great length. I have only ever done the very minimum required of me."

"Regardless, I should like to know what you *can* play," Lady Sophia replied. "It will be helpful when – or if – the time comes for gentlemen to hear you play."

Maria shuddered visibly.

"I pray that will never occur," she answered, before settling her hands on the keys once more and attempting to play – from memory – the only piece she had ever really learned. It was not at all impressive and certainly there were quite a few mistakes and wrong notes, but Lady Sophia, to her credit, did not flinch nor recoil during any part of Maria's performance.

When the last few notes died away, Maria closed her eyes and let out a heavy sigh, knowing all too well that she had made many mistakes.

"You can speak honestly, Lady Sophia," she said, as her friend began to smile. "I know that it is very poor indeed."

"It is not... *terrible*," Lady Sophia answered, her honesty making Maria laugh. "But certainly, if you were ever asked to play for others to hear, it would not be wise to play that particular piece!"

"It is the only one I know – and certainly the one I practiced the most!" Maria protested weakly, as Lady Sophia grinned, her eyes bright with mirth. "Whatever shall I do?"

Lady Sophia considered for a moment, her head tipped to one side.

"Why do you not practice that piece all the more?" she asked, as Maria scowled. "I know that you do not wish to, but if you want to give the impression that you have particular... accomplishments, then you will need to do so." Maria's scowl remained, even though she knew all too well that what Lady Sophia suggested was a wise thought. "And mayhap there will be another piece that I can find for the two of us to play together," Lady Sophia continued, making her way to the small table on which was set a collection of music books. "Or if you can sing whilst I play...?"

She looked up questioningly at Maria, who simply shook her head and rolled her eyes, making Lady Sophia laugh again. The last thing that Maria wanted to do was to be forced to sing for that, she was certain, was even worse than her piano playing!

"Then I will find a suitable duet," Lady Sophia said, with satisfaction. "And, if you *are* asked to play and find yourself entirely unable to do so, then we shall do as I have suggested and see if I cannot play for you, under the guise of turning the pages or some such thing."

"I think that would be rather difficult to enact," Maria mumbled, reluctantly. "I will do my utmost to practice whatever you think I ought, Lady Sophia."

"Even though you would much rather be in my brother's library, I presume?"

Maria sighed and rose from the pianoforte.

"Indeed, Lady Sophia, indeed." She ran one hand carelessly over the top of the pianoforte, her heart a little heavier than before. "But I am quite certain that gentlemen of the *ton* do not wish to court a young lady who has more interest in certain matters than they!" She gave Lady Sophia a wry smile. "And certainly not one who might, in fact, be able to converse about them more knowledgeably than they can!"

"But surely there must be at least *one* gentleman who thinks such characteristics, such interests, are all that he requires in a wife? A gentleman who finds such conversation to be welcoming?"

"I doubt it very much indeed," Maria replied, truthfully. "I have been in London for the Season and again over the autumn and winter and never, as yet, have I had a gentleman show an interest in furthering their acquaintance with me. I wonder now if it was because I was much too free with my opinions in conversation, clearly revealing that I was – that I am – a bluestocking." She shook her head a little sadly. "Therefore, I will set the truth of my character aside and pretend that it is not a part of me for the present."

Lady Sophia set down the music she was holding and came a little closer, her expression one of sympathy.

"I am sorry you feel you must do so, although I am willing and indeed glad to help you."

"There is no need to feel any such sorrow," Maria replied, briskly. "If it is what I must do in order not to become a maiden aunt, then I have every intention of going forward as we have planned." She smiled at Lady Sophia and set aside any niggling doubts or flurries of guilt. "And I am quite certain it will be worth it."

"Lord Bradstock, my Lady."

Maria settled her nerves as she glanced up at the card Lady Hayward now held, relieved that it was not Lord Ridlington who had come to call. There was something about his manner, his conversation, and the like, which left her feeling greatly unsettled indeed. She could not quite place what it was and certainly did not want to experience it any further, given just how much embarrassment she had felt during the ball and their dance together.

It had been a deliberate choice to speak of their first

encounter, of her embarrassment when it had come to her watching him so closely, but it had been in the vain hope that the tension which had spiraled between them ever since their introduction would dissipate. It *had* done so, only to be replaced by another when he had asked her what they ought to discuss instead. She had found herself eager to state that yes, she should very much like to discuss the position of the British Empire at present but, instead, she had forced herself to remain silent and to pretend that she did not understand a word that would have been said to her on the matter. That had brought a pain to her heart, however, a pain which had not quite left her as yet. It was as though she had only just realized what it would be like for her to have to pretend to be another person entirely. It would come at a cost to her, certainly, and might, as Lady Sophia had suggested, be very difficult indeed.

But it will be worth it in the end, she told herself, stoutly. *You must not give up simply because you dislike it so. Not if you want to find the same happiness as your sisters.*

This thought brought with it such a rush of determination that it seemed to force Maria to sit up a little straighter as the butler suddenly reappeared in the doorway, hurrying back towards Lady Hayward once more with what appeared to be *another* card.

"The first gentleman has stated that he is very glad to have the second call at the same time, my Lady," she heard him say as she glanced at Lady Sophia, who gave a very small shrug. "What should I do?"

Lady Hayward chuckled, handing both the cards back to her butler.

"Well, show them both in!" she exclaimed, as he nodded. "And make certain that there is an additional tea tray, given that we are to have two gentlemen calling upon us instead of one!"

"But of course, my Lady," the butler murmured, before hurrying from the room.

"Well, it seems we are to have Lord Bradstock *and* Lord Ridlington calling together," Lady Hayward said, lifting one eyebrow as she looked first at Lady Sophia and then at Maria herself. "They are both eager to see you again, it seems."

Maria forced a smile to her lips, aware of the tightness which had come into her chest the moment that Lady Hayward had mentioned Lord Ridlington.

"How wonderful!" Lady Sophia exclaimed, before casting a slightly doubtful look towards Maria. "I do hope that I will speak well."

"I am certain you shall," Lady Hayward replied, just as Lady Sophia rose to her feet and moved quickly across the room so that she might sit next to Maria. "Come now, there is no time for silliness, Sophia! You need not—"

She was unable to question her daughter further, for a small knock at the door indicated the gentlemen's arrival and Maria rose to her feet, just as Lady Sophia and Lady Hayward did the same. First to enter was Lord Bradstock, with Lord Ridlington close on his heels. They bowed low as Lady Hayward welcomed them and Maria sank into a curtsey, finding her heart quickening all the more as she did so. She felt a reluctance to catch Lord Ridlington's eye, but she forced herself to do so regardless, seeing how he glanced back at her before his gaze shifted to Lady Sophia before returning to Lady Hayward.

Maria let out a long, slow breath, pushing away the tension that nipped at her heart. There was no need for her to feel such a way, to feel such awkwardness or unease. She was, she reminded herself, just as any other young lady of the *ton* would be. She would not mention anything of particular interest to her, such as the Corn Laws or the like, but would keep her conversation light and banal in the hope that this would present her as the sort of young lady society expected.

"Please, do sit down!" Lady Hayward exclaimed as Maria and Lady Sophia returned to their seats. "Do tell us what you thought of the ball last evening, Lord Ridlington. If it was your very first occasion in London society, I must confess myself a little intrigued as to your thoughts!"

Lord Ridlington settled himself in his seat and Maria took a few moments to study him as he spoke. There was a sense of gravitas about him, his dark hair swept back from his forehead, but his eyes, which she knew now to be grey and swirling with almost thunderous clouds, roved from one side of the room to the other. He had a firm jaw and broad shoulders, and whilst not overly tall, certainly seemed to give the impression of a strong, if not somewhat formidable presence. She could not explain what it was about his appearance that had drawn her to study him in such a manner as she had done first at the ball last evening, nor why, even now, she found a faint stirring of interest in her heart.

Is this a gentleman I might find myself willing to consider?

The question slammed into her mind as Lady Hayward and Lady Sophia laughed at something Lord Ridlington had said, leaving Maria attempting to do the same whilst she struggled to find her breath again, such had been the astonishment of the question. Was there more to her sense of embarrassment when it came to Lord Ridlington? Was the reason for such feelings because there was a small urging within her heart towards him? She had never truly felt any such thing before, had never once found herself at all engaged with interest towards a gentleman, and yet now that there was even just a small modicum of it within her heart, Maria found herself quite terrified of it.

"Lady Maria?"

She blushed furiously, recognizing that, having been lost in thought, she had not realized that a question had been directed towards her.

"I should say that Lady Maria will state the same as I," came the voice of Lady Sophia, speaking quite clearly and directly. "That the dances last evening were quite wonderful, although the same could not be said for every gentleman!"

Maria threw a grateful glance towards her friend before turning back to Lord Ridlington, who was looking at her expectantly.

"It is precisely as Lady Sophia says, Lord Ridlington," she replied, forcing a smile to her lips and praying that the warmth in her cheeks would fade soon. "Whilst every dance was enjoyable, some were a little more delightful than others."

Lord Bradstock chuckled, just as the door behind him opened to permit the entry of two maids, who carried trays in their hands.

"I must hope, Lady Maria, that *I* was not one of those gentlemen who you found a little less pleasant than others!"

She smiled back at him, more grateful than ever towards Lady Sophia for helping her back into the conversation without any real embarrassment.

"Of course not, Lord Bradstock," she replied, seeing how Lord Ridlington frowned, clearly worrying now that *he* was one of the gentlemen she spoke of. "Nor you either, Lord Ridlington. Both of our dances were very agreeable indeed, as I am sure Lady Sophia will agree."

Lady Sophia nodded and this brought out yet another chuckle from Lord Bradstock, although Lord Ridlington looked nothing short of relieved.

"And do you intend to step out this evening also?" Lord Ridlington asked, not fixing his gaze upon any one person but looking around at them all. "Are you engaged anywhere particular?"

Lady Hayward nodded.

"We are to attend Lord Penrith's soiree this evening, Lord Ridlington," she answered, as Maria caught sight of Lord Bradstock smiling directly at Lady Sophia, his eyes seemingly fixed to her. "And you?"

"I believe I am engaged there also this evening," he replied, as Maria forced her attention back towards him, not wanting to consider at present what was occurring between Lord Bradstock and Lady Sophia. "I am well acquainted with Lord Penrith. He and I have shared business interests and thus, I have often been in discussion with him about such things." His lips twisted, his brow furrowing for a moment. "Some time ago, there was difficulty with the Luddites which, in return, affected Lord Penrith's business – and my own also, I should say."

"But that has been brought to an end, has it not?" Maria found herself saying, only to receive a sharp nudge from Lady Sophia. Recalling that a young lady of the *beau monde* would not know anything of the Luddite uprising or the consequences that came thereafter, she did her best to cover her remarks quickly. "That is to say, I am certain that Lord Hosmer – who is lately married to my sister – has spoken of such a thing."

Lord Ridlington's eyes had flared wide with surprise at her first remark but now, much to her relief, he appeared to be much more at ease. There was no evident upset in his expression and he nodded sagely, seemingly quite contented with the idea that a young lady would know of matters such as this through the discussion of another gentleman.

"Yes, Lord Hosmer is correct," he said, as Maria let out a quiet breath of relief. "But there have been some long-lasting effects which have gone on to have a particular impact on certain matters of business – although none of this, I am sure, is of any interest to either of you!"

He laughed and Maria forced herself to smile, wishing instead that she could tell him that she would very much like to discuss the matter and to know precisely what difficulties he had encountered. Instead, she remained silent and reached for her teacup, leaving Lord Bradstock and Lady Sophia to converse for a few moments.

"Indeed," she heard Lady Sophia say. "Both myself and Lady Maria play, although I also enjoy singing a great deal."

"I am sure that there will be ample opportunity for you both to step forward and entertain us all this evening," Lord Bradstock said, as Maria took a sip of her tea. "Lord Penrith is very fond of music. I do hope that we will have an opportunity to hear you play, Lady Maria."

She choked on her tea at this remark, doing her utmost to cover it by setting her teacup down and attempting to swallow the tea as best she could. Pulling her handkerchief from her sleeve, she covered her mouth and attempted to cough as delicately as she could, just as tears began to stream from her eyes.

"Good gracious!" Lord Bradstock exclaimed, sitting a little further forward in his chair. "Are you quite all right?"

Lady Sophia was patting Maria gently on the back as she finally managed to swallow her tea, gasping for breath in what was a most unladylike manner.

"I – I do apologize," she said, now dabbing at her eyes with her handkerchief. "Forgive me, please."

Lord Bradstock shook his head, whilst Lord Ridlington's eyes were fixed on Maria's.

"There is nothing you need apologize for, Lady

Maria," Lord Ridlington said, quickly. "You are quite recovered, I hope?"

"I am," she rasped, as Lady Hayward made to move out of her chair, only for Maria to wave her back. "I am quite well, I assure you."

Lord Bradstock and Lord Ridlington seemed to relax just a little at this, although both of them continued to watch her carefully, as though they feared she might start coughing again.

"I do hope you are not unwell, Lady Maria," Lady Hayward remarked, her eyes filled with concern. "It would be a great shame were you to miss this evening's soiree."

"I am sure I shall be very well recovered in a short time," Maria replied, knowing all too well that her face was scarlet with embarrassment. "Forgive me for interrupting your conversation."

She smiled at Lord Ridlington, who merely gave her a long, searching look in response. Without meaning to, Maria found herself looking back at him in return, a little surprised to find her heart quickening in response. It was the same way that she had felt when he had first caught her attention in the hallway, as she had waited to enter the ballroom – that strange curiosity which seemed to pull her towards him seemed to quicken her heart.

"I am sure that our gracious host will understand, once I have explained to him that you are unwell today." Lord Bradstock's deep voice interrupted Maria's gaze and considerations, forcing her attention back towards him rather than continuing to search Lord Ridlington's eyes.

She saw his lips twitch and a flicker of mirth come into his expression. "I would be glad to inform him."

Lady Sophia spread her hands.

"I would agree, Lord Bradstock," she said, as a flush of heat began to creep up Maria's spine, realizing that she had just been caught practically staring at Lord Ridlington, with him watching her in return. "I certainly will be glad to play this evening. Lady Maria perhaps might wish to postpone any such thing, given her delicate state."

Lord Bradstock and Lord Ridlington nodded fervently, as though they were in complete agreement.

"Let us see what this evening brings," Lady Hayward said gently, as Maria prayed desperately that she would not have to do so. "The first thing to do, Lady Maria, is to make certain that you are quite well."

"And therefore, we should take our leave." Lord Ridlington rose to his feet and bowed towards Maria. "I do hope you are fully recovered very soon, Lady Maria."

Maria stood and curtsied, just as Lord Bradstock bowed in order to bid them farewell, although Maria did not miss the way that his eyes turned towards Lady Sophia for a long, lingering look.

"Good afternoon, Lord Bradstock, Lord Ridlington," Maria said, wanting to make it quite plain that she was not struggling in any way with ill health, although if it was going to help remove her from the responsibility of having to play the pianoforte for any assembled group, then she would be glad of it. "Until we see you this evening."

The two gentlemen took their leave but Maria

remained standing, turning to look into the wide eyes of Lady Sophia.

"If you might excuse us, Lady Hayward?" Maria asked as Lady Sophia came to stand beside her. "I think, in light of what has been said, we should attempt to practice before this evening."

Lady Hayward looked a little surprised but, after a moment, nodded.

"But of course."

"Should any other gentlemen or ladies come to call, you will inform us?" Lady Sophia asked, as her mother nodded again. "Thank you, Mama."

Lady Hayward said nothing more but simply watched them depart, making Maria wonder if Lady Hayward had surmised why Maria had been so taken by surprise by the mention of playing the pianoforte this evening.

"Whatever am I to do?" she whispered, as they left the drawing-room. "I will certainly never improve in time for this evening!"

"We will do what we can," Lady Sophia replied, firmly. "Have no fear, Lady Maria. It may be that you will not be called upon this evening. It was foolish of me to speak so."

Maria shook her head.

"Do not berate yourself, Lady Sophia," she answered, firmly. "Come, let us hurry to the music room. There is no time to waste!"

CHAPTER SIX

"Tell me what you know of Lady Maria."

Isaac knew all too well that speaking of Lady Maria to Bradstock would, of course, pique the man's interest, but he had decided that there was no need to hide his intentions. After all, he had been very clear with Bradstock before about all of his many requirements when it came to choosing a bride, so why should he not go on to ask about Lady Maria?

Bradstock chuckled as the carriage rolled away from Lady Hayward's townhouse.

"You have seen her for yourself, have you not?" he asked, as Isaac rolled his eyes. "What else is there that you wish to know? Can you not improve your acquaintance with her a little more so that you discover more about the lady for yourself?"

"I have no time for such things," Isaac replied, a little stiffly. "You know that I have specific..."

"You have a list of demands that must be met by the

lady in question before she is permitted to further her acquaintance with you," Bradstock interrupted, wryly. "Yes, I am well aware of that. It means, I suppose, that you will not be considering Lady Sophia, given that she is in her first Season?"

Isaac scoffed at the thought.

"Of course I shall not be considering her!" he stated, as Bradstock's lips curved into a smile, his gaze turning towards the window. "She is, as you have said, newly come out. Therefore, given that I have already decided that such a creature cannot be a wise choice for a bride, I have not even given her a moment's thought!"

"Even though you are also enjoying your first Season," Bradstock remarked, pointedly. "How very odd that you have such a differing standard for these young ladies compared to yourself."

Opening his mouth to give a retort, Isaac found himself slowly sinking into silence, seemingly unable to answer his friend. Instead, he muttered something indistinct whilst refusing to allow the stab of guilt that came with Bradstock's response to injure him in any way.

"As for Lady Maria," Bradstock continued after a few moments, a glint in his eye which stated that he had been all too aware of Isaac's inability to respond in kind. "She is the daughter of a Duke and therefore, from a very good family."

Isaac's brow furrowed.

"Indeed."

"Which is, I believe one of your requirements, is it not?" Bradstock added as Isaac nodded. "In addition, I am certain that she will have an excellent dowry and inheritance, when the time comes."

"I see," Isaac murmured, not allowing Bradstock's remarks to irritate him any further. He knew what would be best for him and he was not ashamed to have such conditions for any young lady he might consider as more than an acquaintance.

"In addition, from my acquaintance of the lady, I would say that she is very well-spoken, well-mannered, and genteel."

"That does not tell me a great deal about her character," Isaac replied, his frown deepening just a little. "Does she have a calmness about her manner? She is not inclined towards fripperies, I hope?"

Bradstock laughed and threw up his hands.

"I do not know!" he exclaimed, as Isaac grimaced. "If you might recall, I have very little *specific* interest in the many ladies of my acquaintance. I do not attempt to ask them such things, nor do I have any desire to know of them either!" He dropped his hands to his lap and shrugged. "If you wish to discover such things, then I suggest you acquaint yourself a little more with her."

This felt, to Isaac, as though it would be something of a pointless exercise given that he would have to spend a good deal of time with Lady Maria in order to improve his acquaintance with her, only for it then to turn out to be quite useless if she did not satisfy his requirements. But there seemed to be no other way for him to find the answers he currently sought, and thus Isaac had to resign himself to the fact that he would have to do as Bradstock suggested.

"You cannot be thinking that there is something of a *difficulty* in spending time with the lady!" Bradstock exclaimed as Isaac shrugged, not wanting to give an answer. "Good gracious, man! She is a beautiful, eligible young lady who has, so far, presented herself well to you, has she not? Why then would you appear so reluctant?"

Isaac did not immediately answer. The truth was, he was doing his utmost to ignore this strange interest in Lady Maria which had arisen from the very moment he had first set eyes on her and, in being practically minded, he was managing to quash those emotions very well indeed. That was not something he wished to express to Bradstock, however, and thus, he merely shrugged in response.

"You fear that she will not meet your standards and thus, you will have wasted your time," Bradstock muttered, as though he had been able to read the thoughts in Isaac's mind. "Can you not simply enjoy her company, rather than attempt to ascertain whether or not she is suitable?"

"I can do both," Isaac replied, firmly. "I must know her character. If she is not even-tempered, for example, then there is no reason for our acquaintance to continue."

Bradstock sighed heavily and shook his head.

"Might you tell me the extent of your requirements?" he asked, tilting his head just a little and fixing Isaac with what appeared to be a stern gaze. "If there is something that you say, which I know Lady Maria does *not* fulfill, then I might save you the effort that you are seemingly so reluctant to give."

Isaac nodded and settled back in his seat.

"She must be, as I have said, even-tempered," he began, ticking them off on his fingers. "She must be accomplished in the usual attributes that are expected of young ladies."

"You know that she can dance well enough," Bradstock interjected but Isaac's lips twisted in response.

"I do not think that is the only requirement," he stated, firmly. "Besides being able to dance, there should be a proficiency in music, in drawing and the like. Certainly, I would expect her to have excellent manners in all things and to show a particular interest in how she presents herself."

"You mean to say, in the manner of her clothing?"

"Yes, indeed," Isaac replied, without hesitation. "An interest in what one wears speaks of an understanding of one's position."

Bradstock pressed his lips together for some moments but said nothing, gesturing for Isaac to continue as the carriage rolled along.

"When it comes to the servants of the house, she will speak to them with the right degree of civility, showing that she will be able to manage and run my household without difficulty," Isaac continued. "She will understand all matters of etiquette without difficulty."

"For example?" Bradstock asked as Isaac considered for a moment.

"For example, I would not expect the lady to speak to someone across the dinner table from her but instead to make certain to confine conversation to those on either side of her," he said, as Bradstock rolled his eyes, evidently thinking this a little foolish. "And laughter and joviality must be moderated."

"Even though there is no restraint upon gentlemen," Bradstock said emphatically, but Isaac quickly disregarded this, continuing on in earnest with what he expected of any potential bride.

"In addition, I would not expect her to have any interest in, or knowledge of, finance, commerce, or the like." Isaac shook his head to himself, feeling a sense of distaste rising up within him. "I should not like a wife who has any interest at all in such matters."

"You mean to say that you would not abide a bluestocking," Bradstock replied, with a small smile. "I think you will find yourself in company with many a gentleman in that regard, Ridlington."

"And, of course, I would expect nothing but polite conversation and courteous dignity in her behavior and her speech at all times," Isaac finished, dropping his hands to his lap. "She should not be too familiar and certainly never flirtatious! I could not abide such behavior from a lady of society!" He shook his head, as Bradstock chuckled. "Not even a hint of vulgarity to come from her, no outbursts of laughter or displays of emotion can ever be permitted."

"And you should not like to hear her opinion on certain matters," Bradstock finished, stating what was all too well known to be a very much frowned upon behavior amongst those in society. "I think we differ in that regard, Ridlington."

Isaac spread his hands.

"I should not like to hear her opinion upon *any* matter, unless I ask for her to express it directly!" he exclaimed, as Bradstock sighed and looked out of the window again. "You know very well that society does not expect or even *allow* ladies of the *ton* to –"

"But how will you ever know what the lady thinks or feels if you do not ask her or permit her to express such things?" Bradstock asked, interrupting Isaac, his eyes searching Isaac's face.

"I – I do not see a requirement for it," Isaac replied, speaking with a little more uncertainty as Bradstock let out a bark of laughter. "There is no need to know one's wife in such depth, surely?" He shrugged as Bradstock closed his eyes in evident disbelief. "Marriage is simply to produce one's heir and, thereafter, can provide companionship and the like, but that does not require any depth of intimacy."

Bradstock opened his eyes and gave Isaac what appeared to be a very bewildered look indeed.

"I do not think I shall ever understand your way of thinking, Ridlington," he stated, as the carriage began to slow. "When the time comes for me to choose a bride, I will do all that I can to ensure that I know everything about her. I will be eager to know her thoughts and opinions on certain matters. I will want to know what she feels, in the hope that perhaps our hearts might fill with a gentle affection for each other which will bring our marriage into excellent standing."

"Affection?" Isaac snorted, thinking the idea to be more than a little ridiculous. "I do not think there is any need whatsoever for such a thing. That is the very *least* of my concerns!"

Tilting his head, Bradstock looked back at Isaac steadily, just as the footman pulled open the carriage door in preparation for them to alight.

"Then might I ask, is your interest in Lady Maria solely to do with the fact that you think her able to fulfill all that you have set out as regards your future bride?"

"Yes, of course," Isaac lied, ignoring the stab of guilt which lanced his heart. "There is nothing more to my interest in her than that."

Bradstock's smile was lopsided, his eyes twinkling as he continued to hold Isaac's gaze.

"Then you do not find her beautiful?" he asked, pointedly. "There is nothing about her that draws you to her? Nothing that might encourage even a flicker of interest in your heart?"

Isaac took in a deep breath but shook his head.

"Nothing whatsoever," he replied, firmly, even though he knew all too well that the precise opposite was true. "Yes, she is very beautiful indeed, but that is merely something I consider to be expected in whomever I then go on to choose as my bride."

A muttered exclamation left Bradstock's mouth as he made his way out of the carriage, leaving Isaac to follow after him. Isaac was not quite certain why but, evidently, he had irritated Bradstock in some way. Mentally shrugging, he climbed out after his friend and stood in the sunshine.

"I will see you this evening, then," he said, as Bradstock nodded, choosing, it seemed, not to say anything.

"And I shall attempt to further my acquaintance with Lady Maria, just as you have suggested."

Bradstock sighed and looked away.

"I do hope you are successful," he said, glancing back at Isaac, his lips twitching for a moment. "In fact, no, I do *not* wish you success!"

A little surprised, Isaac stared at Bradstock, not at all understanding what his friend meant.

"I hope that you will find yourself desperately in love with the lady and that you will not know what to do," Bradstock continued, his hand reaching out to slam down on Isaac's shoulder. "That these ideas you hold, these standards that you expect your wife to reach, will be thrown down asunder and you will find yourself completely and utterly confused." He grinned and pulled his hand away. "What say you to that, Ridlington?"

"I think it utterly impossible," Isaac replied, firmly, as Bradstock chuckled. "Good afternoon, Bradstock."

"Good afternoon, Ridlington," came the reply. "I do hope this evening goes well!"

DESPITE WHAT HE had said to Bradstock, Isaac was all too aware of the sense of anticipation which rose within him as he entered Lord Penrith's drawing-room. It did not come simply from being in amongst society again, but rather from the awareness that Lady Maria would be present. The fact that he had spoken to Bradstock about her made it all the more certain in his mind that she was, in fact, a lady who might very well fulfill all that he required. To have discovered a lady so soon after entering society was, to Isaac, a very great blessing indeed, although he was still quite aware that she might end up being not all that he required.

And you have to confess that there is a flickering interest in your heart when it comes to the lady.

Isaac grimaced and ignored the quiet voice of his conscience in his head. He did not want to talk to Bradstock about such things and certainly did not want to even admit it to himself! There was, as he had stated earlier, no thought of developing any sort of affection with the lady in question, nor with any other than might step into his regard. There was no need for it, for it would surely only complicate matters! Therefore, Isaac was quietly determined to rid himself of this strange interest in Lady Maria, one way or the other. Even if she *was* to prove herself entirely suitable, even if he did end up seeking to betroth himself to her, there was still no thought of affection. The sort of marriage he sought was an entirely practical one and that was all he required.

"Good evening, Lord Ridlington!"

Isaac quickly recognized Lady Forester and bowed low, smiling back at her as she curtsied.

"Good evening, Lady Forester," he replied, before quickly greeting her daughter, Miss Fawkes.

This was then followed by swift introductions to those who stood with Lady Forester, meaning that Isaac was drawn into conversation for some time. He was glad of it, however, for it meant that the number of his acquaintances was increasing all the more quickly, and he would need that, should Lady Maria turn out to be less than he hoped.

The evening passed quickly and Isaac made his way around the room, speaking to various acquaintances and finding himself introduced to many more. As yet, however, he had not seen Lady Maria and was irritated to find a nudge of alarm in his chest. When the host caught the attention of all of his guests and stated that there was to be some musical performances, however, Isaac quickly spotted Lady Maria and Lady Sophia standing together, for the rest of the guests moved forward with haste whilst they remained behind.

He smiled to himself, choosing to make his way into the music room and taking a chair near to Bradstock, who acknowledged him with a small smile and a murmur of greeting. Isaac let himself watch the doorway, his gaze fixed on those who came inside. Near to the very end came Lady Sophia and Lady Maria, with Lady Hayward following. Had they come in near to the end in the hope that they would be seen, would be noticed by the host and, thereafter, asked to play? He had thought that there was an eagerness there when he and Bradstock had called upon them both earlier that day – certainly from Lady Sophia, at least. Lady Maria had endured that awful coughing episode although, had she not been struck down so, he was certain that she would have said the very same. Seeing Lord Penrith making his way around the room, talking quietly to every guest, Isaac waited until his host came near to him before he spoke.

"An excellent evening, Lord Penrith!" he exclaimed, as Lord Penrith smiled and thanked him. "I am sure we will be very well entertained with whoever is to play or sing for us this evening."

"I am certain we shall be," Lord Penrith replied with a smile. "I am glad you are come to London, Lord Ridlington. It is a delight to have you join society at last!"

Isaac smiled, recalling the many conversations he had shared with Lord Penrith about whether or not he would come to join the London Season at any time. Of course, Isaac had been entirely determined to make certain that his estate was profitable and that any business matters had been dealt with before he even considered coming to London - and he had made that quite clear to Lord Penrith - but now he found himself very glad indeed to be present this evening, amongst the *beau monde*.

"I am sure," he said, lowering his voice just a little, "that Lady Sophia and Lady Maria would be very pleased indeed if you should call upon them to play."

"Oh?" Lord Penrith asked as Isaac nodded.

"I called upon them both earlier this afternoon and certainly, they both seemed quite eager," he said, ignoring the fact that Lady Maria had been so overcome to the point that she could not have answered. "I have never heard either of them play."

Lord Penrith looked quite satisfied.

"Then I shall beg for their favor," he replied, putting one hand on Isaac's shoulder for a moment. "Thank you for your insight, Lord Ridlington. It can often be difficult to find the *first* young lady who might be willing to play, but the moment that the first performance is at an end, they all seem very eager indeed!" He chuckled and lifted his hand. "I shall go to them directly. Thank you, Ridlington. Enjoy the rest of the evening."

"I will," Isaac replied, sitting back in his chair and feeling quite satisfied indeed. "And I thank you, Lord Penrith. Good evening."

CHAPTER SEVEN

O*ne week later*

MARIA SQUINTED AT HER WORK, trying to see how she might improve it. Lady Sophia stood stock still in front of Maria, her chin lifted towards the window where soft light came pouring through. It danced around her and made for a very fine picture indeed – but Maria simply could not capture it, no matter how hard she tried.

"It is of no use!" she exclaimed, as Lady Sophia dropped her hands with a sigh of relief and made to step a little closer to her. "I cannot achieve it."

"I am certain you can," Lady Sophia replied, coming towards her. "Now, why do you not show me what you have done thus far?"

Maria sighed and shook her head, feeling already far too much embarrassment given the poor drawing she had done.

"I am already far too ashamed," she stated, only for Lady Sophia to laugh and reach for the paper, looking at it with a careful eye.

"You – you have tried, certainly, to capture my pose," she said, evidently struggling to find something to say. "Have you ever attempted to paint with watercolors?"

Maria laughed and dropped her pencil to the table.

"I hardly think that, if I cannot draw, I will have any ability to paint!" she said, as Lady Sophia allowed herself a tiny smile. "You need not worry or seek to improve me further, Lady Sophia. I am quite contented with my lack of success."

Lady Sophia's lips twisted, her expression a little forlorn.

"I am sure that I could–"

"*Please*," Maria replied, grasping Lady Sophia's hand and squeezing her fingers gently. "There is nothing more than needs to be said. I have not the skill nor the talent and feel no shame because of it."

She smiled at Lady Sophia, who let out a huff of breath, her brows knotting.

"And what if Lord Ridlington one day asks for you to draw him something of great importance?" Lady Sophia asked, one eyebrow now lifting into a gentle arch. "What then?"

Maria hesitated, then shrugged.

"I do not think that such a thing will ever occur," she replied, ignoring the twist of her stomach at the mention of Lord Ridlington's name. "Why ever should you think so?"

Lady Sophia laughed, her hands settling gently on her hips.

"You must think I am very foolish indeed if you believe that I am not at all aware of Lord Ridlington's interest in your company!"

Maria was about to protest, but knew she could not, for to do so would only be attempting to hide what had become more than obvious to her also. Lord Ridlington had called upon them both almost every day, had sought her out during social occasions, and had generally been very attentive indeed. He had many questions, however, and Maria had found it difficult to hide the truth of what she thought and felt from him. In addition, she had been all the more unsettled to realize that there was a flicker of interest in her heart which was growing steadily. In fact, it was more than just a flicker. Now, it was a flame. A flame which ignited the moment that she woke and would not leave her heart no matter what she attempted. What was worse, it continued to grow every time she was in his company and, given that he was in her company practically every day, her consideration of him grew steadily.

"He may very well be interested in my company, Lady Sophia, but he will certainly not be interested in my drawings!" she replied, trying to push a little levity into their conversation and choosing to say nothing of what was growing within her heart. "Please, you need not worry about my lack of skill in this particular medium. You have already been a help to me and I feel as though there is nothing at all I have done in response."

"How can you say such a thing?" Lady Sophia protested as Maria scrunched up her poor attempt at drawing a portrait of Lady Sophia, before throwing it into the fireplace, quite contented for it to be used to set a fire whenever it was next needed. "You have assisted me a great deal!"

"I have done no such thing!" Maria replied, laughing. "I have stood by your side and mayhap have made one or two encouraging remarks, but that is all."

Lady Sophia shook her head.

"No, indeed, I shall not permit you to think so poorly of yourself. You have done more than that. Whenever we have been out in society, you have taken great pains to mention to me the gentlemen and the ladies whom you are already acquainted with, and have been more than willing to inform me as to whether or not they are worth improving my acquaintance with. Also, you have stepped into the conversation at times, when I have said something a little foolish or untoward –"

"As you have done for me also," Maria interjected, but Lady Sophia continued on regardless, as though she had not heard her.

"You have saved me from embarrassment and shown me an example of how one acts within society which has been more than a little helpful."

Maria did not smile at this remark, however, shaking her head as she did so.

"I have done very little," she insisted. "And I fear that I have done very poorly when it comes to conversation and the like, for I have been very stilted in my remarks and not at all as I would usually have been."

Her lips twisted as she recalled how, only yesterday, she had forced herself to remain entirely silent when the three gentlemen within their group had been speaking of the Corn Laws and she had eagerly wanted to involve herself in their discussion. Had it been last Season, then she would have done so. But this Season, in her attempts to make a change, she had stayed silent and had feigned ignorance. She had even laughed and smiled when one of the other ladies had berated the gentlemen for speaking of things that excluded them entirely, given that they had no knowledge of such matters! Maria had despised herself for doing so but, as much as she wished it were not so, it seemed that her silence and her more reserved nature were having the desired effect. She had danced more this last sennight than she had ever done before, and gentlemen were seemingly glad to make conversation with her and had begun seeking her out at the various occasions they had attended. She had not only enjoyed Lord Ridlington's company, but also three other gentlemen who had called upon her this last sennight. There had also been Lord Bradstock, who had been dutiful in his calls but who Maria suspected came to visit Lady Sophia more than she. Whether or not Lady Sophia was entirely aware of his interest as yet, she did not know, but certainly, she was more than inclined to say something if Lady Sophia herself did not bring him into conversation soon!

"Does this mean that you do not wish to continue with our guise?" Lady Sophia asked as Maria shook her head fervently. "You would like to continue?"

"So long as I am not asked to play the pianoforte

again," Maria muttered, drawing a smile from Lady Sophia. "That was almost entirely disastrous!"

Lady Sophia waved one hand.

"No indeed, it was not," she stated, picking up Maria's pencil and, turning so that she might look at the scene before her, beginning to sketch lightly on a fresh piece of paper. "It was a little embarrassing, of course, to be asked so directly, but I thought you did very well."

Maria closed her eyes, already blocking out the memory of what had occurred. Lord Penrith had been very eager indeed as he had approached them both, stating quite openly that Lord Ridlington had said that he thought both she and Lady Sophia would be very glad to be asked to play for them that evening. It had been frankly impossible for Maria to refuse and thus, she had been forced to rise to her feet and make her way to the pianoforte, with Lady Sophia by her side. There had been no time to discuss what they were to do and therefore, only by whispers, had Lady Sophia managed to explain that she would play and Maria would turn the pages. They had played two pieces together – with Maria feigning her performance for the second piece – whilst Lady Sophia had sung beautifully. She had prayed that no-one would notice her lack of skill and, thankfully, no-one seemed to have done so. However, Lord Penrith had then gone on to ask her, in front of the assembled guests, whether she wished to play alone for a few minutes and Maria had struggled to answer, looking straight ahead and seeing Lord Ridlington's smiling face. She had known that *he* had been the one to suggest such a thing to

Lord Penrith and, for whatever reason, had been eager to hear her play alone. She had declined, however, her face crimson with embarrassment as Lady Sophia had returned to her seat. She had stated that she did not wish to take the place of one of the many other young ladies whom, she was certain, would play a good deal better than she. Of course, there had been murmurs of protest but no-one had spoken out directly and Maria had managed to slip away and return to sit by Lady Sophia, her face flaming still as finally, another young lady rose to take her place at the pianoforte.

Maria desperately hoped that such a thing would not happen again.

"Sophia?"

The sound of Lady Hayward's voice caught both her own and Sophia's attention and they turned at once to see Lady Hayward coming into the music room.

"I just thought to remind you that it will soon be time for afternoon calls," Lady Hayward said, smiling first at her daughter and then at Maria. "If you wish to change, then now would be the most appropriate time."

Maria nodded, glad that her drawing had already been hidden away in the grate for fear that Lady Hayward would see it and be forced to hide her mirth.

"I will change," she said, looking down at her hands and realizing, much to her shame, that she needed to clean her fingers from where she had smudged the pencil lines on her drawing. Inadvertently, of course. "And then I will come directly to the parlor."

"Wonderful," Lady Hayward replied, as Lady Sophia

continued to sketch. "I will see you both again shortly, then."

~

"I DO VERY much enjoy dancing, yes."

Maria dared not glance at Lady Sophia for fear that the look on her face might make her laugh out loud. Lord Brookmire was very persistent, for he had called upon them both almost every day this last week but, unfortunately, their conversation always seemed to flow around the same topics. Maria was quite certain that he had asked her if she enjoyed dancing only yesterday, and Lady Sophia the day before, and, of course, they both answered in the positive.

"I am glad to hear it!" Lord Brookmire boomed, his face a little red as he beamed at her. "You must enjoy balls especially!"

"Indeed I do," Maria replied, knowing all too well what Lord Brookmire's next question would be and deciding to answer it in advance of him even speaking it. "Lady Sophia enjoys balls also and I believe her favorite dance is the cotillion." She glanced at Lady Sophia, whose cheeks had gone very red indeed as she did her utmost to hide her smile. "I would say that I prefer the country dance myself." Looking back at him, she tilted her head and smiled. "And you, Lord Brookmire? What would be your favorite dance?"

Lord Brookmire looked a little taken aback, his eyes wide as he stammered for an answer. A quiet cough came from Lady Hayward and Maria pressed her lips together in an attempt to suppress her own laughter. She knew that she was not behaving particularly well, but Lord Brookmire did not appear to notice.

"I – I would say the supper dance," he replied, after a moment. "For then I am able to engage in conversation with the lady for a good length of time rather than merely enjoying a dance together."

"That is a very kind thought," Lady Hayward said, just as a scratch came at the door. In a moment, the butler had joined them, handing Lady Hayward two cards. Maria saw Lord Brookmire's eyes rest on them for a moment before he rose to his feet, clearly aware that it was time for him to take his leave.

"Do excuse me," he said, bowing to Lady Hayward as the ladies all rose to their feet. "I shall take my leave of you now so that I do not outstay my welcome!"

He smiled at her and Maria curtsied, glad that he did not appear to linger in his gaze. Rather, he turned to bid good afternoon to Lady Sophia and then took his leave just as the butler did so also.

"Lady Maria, I should chide you!" Lady Hayward stated, although as Maria turned to look at her chaperone, she saw the twinkle in the lady's eye. "Lord Brookmire is a very nice gentleman who –"

"Who speaks of the same thing every time he calls, mama!" Lady Sophia protested as Lady Hayward smiled despite herself. "Surely you cannot suggest that Lady Maria nor I am glad of his continued company?"

Lady Hayward sighed and then shook her head.

"Indeed, my dear," she replied, quietly. "As I have said before, my only desire for you both is that you find a gentleman who suits you very well indeed, and who ignites a particular interest within your heart." She lifted one hand and then let it fall. "If Lord Brookmire does neither, then I cannot ask you to encourage his interest. Indeed, I would not!"

Maria smiled and murmured her thanks, only for the door to open again and Lord Ridlington to come to join them, swiftly followed by Lord Bradstock.

"Good afternoon, Lord Bradstock, Lord Ridlington," Lady Hayward said, as they all curtsied. "How good of you to call upon us."

The two gentlemen bowed and Lady Hayward begged them to sit down, before going to ring the bell for yet another tea tray. Maria glanced at Lady Sophia and noticed that she was smiling gently towards Lord Bradstock, her cheeks a little pink. Lord Bradstock was looking directly back at Lady Sophia, a smile playing about his lips also. Maria noted this with interest, determined to speak to her friend about Lord Bradstock just as soon as there was an opportunity.

"And what have you both been doing this fine day?" Lord Bradstock asked as both gentlemen sat down together. "It is a very lovely day indeed. Have you been out of doors yet?"

Lady Sophia shook her head.

"Indeed, we have not," she answered, glancing at Maria who instantly saw the warning in her eyes. "Last evening was very busy indeed and so it was important for us to rest."

Maria nodded and said something about how she had been very fatigued after last night's ball, realizing that if they said anything about their attempts at drawing and the like, Lord Ridlington and Lord Bradstock might express more interest in the subject. "Therefore, Lady Sophia and I have enjoyed a very quiet morning," she finished, just as the maid came in with the tea tray.

"But that has not prevented them from being industrious," Lady Hayward added, gesturing for Sophia to serve the tea. "They have been very busy this morning, have you not, ladies?"

A tight smile crossed Maria's face as she saw both gentlemen look at her with curiosity, knowing now that she had no other choice but to mention what they had been doing.

"Indeed," she said, with a slight shrug. "It was nothing of particular difficulty, however."

"Here, Lord Bradstock," Lady Sophia interrupted, rising to set Lord Bradstock's cup and saucer down before him. "And Lord Ridlington? I presume you would like a cup also?"

Lord Ridlington nodded and thanked her but did not, much to Maria's frustration, change the conversation.

"Might I enquire what you were engaged in?" he asked, as Lady Sophia's attempts to interrupt them with more tea failed entirely. "It is good to find something with which to engage oneself, I think."

Seeing that there was nothing more for her to say other than the truth, Maria threw a quick glance towards Lady Sophia before she spoke.

"Lady Sophia and I were attempting to improve our drawing," she replied, as brightly as she could. "That is all. It was a very bright morning and the light was quite perfect."

She smiled and picked up her teacup, taking a small sip and praying that nothing more would be said.

"Indeed?" Lord Ridlington said, sharing a glance with Lord Bradstock – a look which said a great deal, even though Maria could not understand what was meant by it. "I should very much like to see what you have achieved this morning, Lady Maria."

Maria hesitated, her cup halfway to her mouth as she looked directly back at Lord Ridlington. He had not asked to see Lady Sophia's work, she noticed, as a tightness took hold of her chest. It was not as though she could easily refuse either, for what young lady would *not* be eager to share such things with a gentleman who asked? It was a sign of particular interest, she knew, and yet the thought of having to go and pick up her crumpled piece of paper and set it out before both gentlemen brought nothing but dread to her heart.

"But – but of course," she found herself saying, looking to Lady Hayward in the hope that she might refuse, only to see her chaperone nodding her consent. "If you will excuse me."

Rising to her feet, she threw a desperate glance towards Lady Sophia, who also set her tea aside.

"Do you recall where you set your piece, Lady Maria?" Lady Sophia asked, smiling brightly at Maria. "I believe I set it aside. Let me join you as you look for it."

Grateful, Maria nodded, and together, the two young ladies excused themselves.

"Whatever am I to do?" Maria whispered desperately, as they stepped out into the hallway. "The piece I drew ended up being thrown into the fireplace! You were very kind indeed to speak of it as you did, but I am fully aware of just how dire it was."

"Have no fear," Lady Sophia replied, encouragingly. "I drew a little before my mother came to call us. You shall simply take my piece and present it as your own."

For whatever reason, even though Maria knew very well that this was the perfect solution, a deep sense of guilt plunged into her heart. She gave herself a slight shake as Lady Sophia led her back into the room where they had been drawing and quickly found the sketch she had been working on. It was simply of the scene before them, with a small table to one side with a vase of flowers upon it as the light streamed in from the window to their left. It was very basic but certainly a good deal better than Maria herself could do.

"Here." Lady Sophia handed it to Maria with a broad smile. "I believe Lord Ridlington is very interested in furthering his acquaintance with you, Lady Maria." Her eyes twinkled. "Would you ever consider him?"

Maria hesitated, looking down at the picture and then back at Lady Sophia who was still watching her closely.

"And what of Lord Bradstock?" she asked, choosing to ask another question rather than answer what had been said to her. "I am quite certain that he comes solely to further his acquaintance with you, even though we are both present." She laughed as Lady Sophia blushed, pushing aside any lingering sense of guilt. "Come now, we should return... before *both* Lord Bradstock and Lord Ridlington miss our company!"

Lady Sophia shook her head and murmured something Maria could not quite make out, making her laugh again. They walked back to the drawing-room together, a great sense of relief filling Maria's chest as she held the picture securely in her hand. At least she would not have to endure the embarrassment of showing her original piece to the gentleman and, she decided, any guilt could be easily set aside. Hopefully, Lord Ridlington would be satisfied with what he saw and, given that she did not think he would ever ask to see such a piece again, one single occasion would not be a particularly serious matter. With much increased confidence, Maria stepped back into the drawing-room and resumed her seat, seeing Lady Hayward's smile.

"It is only a light sketch of what was before us," she said, the lie tripping off her tongue easily, even though the words stabbed shame into her heart. "Pray do not judge me too harshly for it!"

Lord Ridlington rose and took the paper from her with a murmur of thanks before sitting back down again. Both he and Lord Bradstock looked at the sketch as Maria sat quietly, not daring to look at either Lady Sophia or Lady Hayward for fear of what she might see in their faces.

"It certainly is promising, Lady Maria."

Lord Ridlington looked up at her and smiled, leaving Maria feeling almost weak with relief.

"I should very much like to see it finished, once you have had time to do so," he continued, as Maria inclined her head in what she hoped was a gracious manner. "I believe you draw very well, Lady Maria."

"Thank you," she answered, as the paper was rolled up and handed back to her. "You are both very kind."

The conversation soon traveled onto further matters, leaving Maria and Lady Sophia to glance at each other in relief. For the moment, it seemed, their deception had been a success.

CHAPTER EIGHT

Isaac looked back at his reflection in the mirror and drew in a deep breath, setting his shoulders as he did so. This was to be his first outing with Lady Maria and, the truth was, he was a little nervous. It was not, he assured himself, because he had any particular *feelings* for the lady, but rather simply because this was not something he had ever undertaken before. He recalled as he adjusted his cravat minutely, the moment he had asked Lady Maria to join him for a short walk in the park. He had seen her eyes widen for a moment and frissons of surprise had entered her expression, only for her to drop her head and thank him quietly, stating just how much she would enjoy such a thing.

The sense of relief and gladness which had filled his heart had surprised him, he had to admit. To be so pleased with her acceptance had been one thing, but he had not been able to remove the delight which seemed to spread through his being. In fact, it had remained with him until this very moment, where it slowly began to be replaced with a quiet nervousness.

"She satisfies all that I require, thus far at least," he told his reflection, his grey eyes a little grave. "I am doing nothing more than determining whether or not there are parts to her character that are somewhat lacking."

His decision to ask her to join him for a short walk around the park had been made the moment he had seen her sketch. Not only could she play the pianoforte; she could also draw rather well. It had not been anything close to completion, but he had expressed an interest in seeing the final piece and was looking forward to admiring it when it was, at last, finished. In addition, he thought Lady Maria to be very amiable indeed but, much to his satisfaction, was not at all inclined to speak overtly about her own opinion, had no interest in matters of business or the like and, thus far, seemed to be quietly contented to speak of nothing other than balls, soirees and the like. Isaac smiled to himself, recalling how she had once mentioned her interest in the various fashion plates which were, of course, of the greatest interest to the ladies of society. Lady Maria certainly always looked very well indeed and Isaac no longer had any difficulty in stating aloud that he found her very lovely. That was, of course, just a practical thought, however. He did not need to give any further thought to what was going on within his heart. That was best quashed and hidden away, just as he had been doing every day these last two weeks. To have any feelings for the lady was not required.

"Very good."

Lifting his chin, Isaac took in a deep breath and then

made his way from the room and down the stairs towards his waiting carriage. He prayed that this afternoon would go well and that Lady Maria would continue to impress him. To have spent so much time in her company only to discover that she was, in fact, unable to fulfill all that he required would be a great disappointment.

Your heart would be very painful indeed, came the quiet voice of his conscience but Isaac batted it away at once. He might be a little frustrated that he had spent so long in a lady's company when she was now no longer suitable, but there would be nothing to be done but to continue regardless. He would simply have to look for another young lady instead if it came to that. He looked out of the carriage window and ignored the wave of tension which washed over him at the very thought of having to step away from Lady Maria.

I feel nothing for her, he told himself, firmly, believing that, if he told himself those words often enough, he might be able to rid himself of the unsettling emotions which were bound deep within his heart. To permit himself to feel the full force of them would not be wise, and Isaac was quite determined not to allow it.

"THERE IS a great deal of beauty here, is there not?"

Isaac looked down at Lady Maria as they walked together through the park, seeing the gentle smile which curved her lips, and noting how the curls which had escaped from the confines of her bonnet to brush across her temples seemed to be burnished with gold. His heart turned over in his chest and he looked away, clearing his throat as he did so, as though such an action might help him regain a little more composure.

"Indeed," he said, a little tightly. "The view is very pleasant indeed."

They said nothing more for some minutes, simply walking together through the park with Lady Hayward a short distance behind, making certain to maintain all propriety. Isaac found himself a little confused, struggling to understand why their conversation appeared to be so lackluster, why he could not find something to say which would bring about a better conversation. His chest felt tight, constricted, and his breathing was certainly a little faster than before. The more he struggled to think of what to say, the more his heart quickened and, much to his frustration, his tongue seemed to stick to the roof of his mouth so that even the thought of speaking aloud was a very difficult one indeed.

"Might I ask if you enjoyed Lord Sheffield's dinner party, Lord Ridlington?"

Lady Maria was the first to break the silence, her green eyes looking up at him for a moment or two before she turned her head away again, looking back towards the path.

"I – I did, yes," Isaac stammered, berating himself silently for being evidently unable to speak in a calm and controlled manner. "I found it to be an exceptional evening."

Lady Maria laughed softly, making him frown as he looked back at her.

"I thought it a little dull, I confess," she said, his

frown burrowing a little more deeply into his forehead as she continued to speak. "But then, mayhap I was not as blessed with good conversation as you, Lord Ridlington."

Isaac considered this for a moment, recalling how Lady Maria had been sitting between Lord Whittemore and Miss Brixton. She had not attempted to speak to anyone other than those who were on either side of her, just as he would have expected from a lady of quality, but did that mean that she had endured poor conversation?

"Lord Whittemore was not inclined towards good conversation?" he asked, only to suddenly remember that Lord Whittemore had drunk a great deal of brandy in the parlor before they all went in to dinner. It had been something of an embarrassment to see the gentleman continue to drink more and more as the evening had gone on, to the point that Lord Whittemore had eventually become so foxed that Lord Sheffield had been required to order two of his footmen to help the gentleman into his carriage for Lord Whittemore had been unable even to stand on his own. Isaac had been glad that the ladies had retired from the table by then, for to have seen such a thing would have caused the greatest mortification for everyone present.

"I am afraid he was not, Lord Ridlington," came Lady Maria's reply, her tone a little sharper than before. "I found him to be most improper, in fact. And Miss Brixton, who sat on my other side, was very quiet indeed." She glanced up at him. "Something of a mouse, in fact."

Silently, Isaac noted Miss Brixton's name and the quiet demeanor that Lady Maria had mentioned. Should he ever be required to consider another young lady, he would not permit himself to go to Miss Brixton, for he did not want to have a wife who remained almost silent whilst he attempted to find something to say. No, in that regard, Lady Maria was quite perfect. She spoke well and was, it seemed, able to make conversation even when he was struggling!

His heart lifted and he found himself smiling at her, all the more gratified when she returned it with a gentle smile of her own, her eyes seeming to sparkle just a little as she held his gaze for a moment. A rush of heat seemed to warm him through as he looked back at her, a little confused as to why he could not seem to pull his gaze away. A sense of contentment rushed through him, a long breath escaping him as Lady Maria looked away from him and back towards the path, a smile still lingering on both of their faces. His shoulders settled and any lingering tension seemed to be blown away on the gentle breeze which brushed between them. Isaac found that his smile remained as they walked together, discovering there to be a strange sense of satisfaction growing steadily within his heart, as though walking beside Lady Maria was all that he required for his heart to find such serenity. His list of requirements, the one he had been attempting to make certain Lady Maria now fulfilled, was pushed from his thoughts as she began to speak of the ball which they would attend tomorrow evening. He listened to her as she talked of Lord and Lady Trailstone, telling him how she had been acquainted with Lady Trailstone *before* she had been wed the previous Season and how she had been so very glad to hear of her engagement to Lord Trailstone.

"She is a very kind lady," Lady Maria finished. "And I believe Lord Trailstone to be an exceptional gentleman."

Isaac resisted the urge to ask her outright if she thought *him* to be an exceptional gentleman, giving himself a slight shake at even the thought of asking such a foolish thing. What did it matter if she thought well of him or not? If they were to court, if they were to wed, then he would expect Lady Maria to have respect for him, similar to that which he would, in return, give to her. Aside from that, he needed nothing more.

Or did he?

"I do hope you will dance with me come the morrow," he found himself saying, his voice a little gruffer than before. "I will seek you out, of course, but I have become aware that, if I do not make my way to your side just as soon as possible, your dance card will already be full!"

Lady Maria laughed and she looked back up at him with a bright smile on her face.

"It was not always so, Lord Ridlington," she said, surprising him with that particular remark. "But given that you are the *first* gentleman to ask me such a thing, I will promise to keep a dance available for you."

"Two, if you please," Isaac replied, before he could stop himself. "I should like to dance with you twice, Lady Maria – if that would be agreeable to you."

Something shifted in Lady Maria's expression. Her smile faded just a little and the brightness in her eyes began to dim. The way she looked back at him, the way she practically studied him, made Isaac feel as though she were searching his very heart, desperate to find an answer which he was already willing to give if only she would ask her question.

"That would be very satisfactory indeed, Lord Ridlington," Lady Maria replied, after a moment or two. "Might I ask which ones you would like me to hold for you?"

Her voice was softer now, speaking with a greater sense of interest than had ever been there before. It was as though she was now beginning to realize that he had more interest in her company than he had ever expressed previously and that, in the moments she had looked up at him and studied him silently, she was deciding what would be best to do.

"Shall we say the quadrille and the waltz?" he asked, his voice a little hoarse as he realized the significance of what he asked. "I would be very grateful indeed if you would keep those two dances for me, Lady Maria."

She held his gaze steadily again for a few moments, their steps slowing as they simply looked back at each other, before finally, she nodded and dropped her eyes back to the path.

"I should be glad to do so, Lord Ridlington," she replied, in that gentle manner that he had come to know so well. "Thank you for your kind consideration."

"Not at all," he blustered, feeling such a swell of relief, gladness, and happiness all mingling together and crushing his heart that he wanted to pause for a moment simply to regain his countenance. "I look forward to it, Lady Maria."

She smiled at him and the gentle glow in her eyes made his breath catch.

"As do I, Lord Ridlington," she told him. "I will remember to do so the very moment I am given my dance card."

Greatly satisfied, Isaac hesitated for just a moment before he offered Lady Maria his arm.

"I think we should return to the carriage now," he said, as she looked from his face to his arm and back again. "The sun is hot and I should not like you to become fatigued."

Lady Maria blinked rapidly and then, after a moment, accepted his arm without question. When he looked down, he could see the way that her pulse beat rapidly in her throat and realized that she was just as caught up in this strange wonderfulness that surrounded them as he was. This brought even more of a lightness to his heart and Isaac felt as though he were walking taller than ever before as they returned to the waiting carriage.

"YOU LOOK A LITTLE TROUBLED."

Isaac shook his head, one hand slamming down on Bradstock's shoulder.

"Indeed, I am not," he replied, as the music from the ballroom swam through the crowd, making its way towards Isaac and Bradstock. "I am not troubled," he answered, as Lord Penrith stepped away, their conversation now at an end. "I assure you."

Bradstock did not look entirely convinced, looking back at Isaac with a troubled gaze.

"Have you discovered something in Lady Maria's character that does not satisfy you?" he asked, as Isaac frowned. "I know that to step away from her now would prove something of a difficulty."

Isaac waved a hand, shaking his head as he did so.

"Indeed not!" he exclaimed, as his eyes alighted on the very young lady that he spoke of. "Lady Maria and I took a short walk in the park yesterday and I found nothing untoward at all."

Bradstock's brows lifted in evident surprise, although Isaac could not quite understand why.

"Indeed," came the reply. "Well, I must say that I am very glad to hear it."

"The reason you find me a little...." Isaac searched for the right word, "a little frustrated, mayhap, is solely to do with the news that harvests this year have been particularly poor. Lord Penrith came to speak to me of his estate," he continued, turning so that he and Bradstock might make their way towards Lady Maria. "I was disheartened to hear of his difficulties."

There was no time to explain further, for Lady Maria, Lady Hayward and Lady Sophia were near to them now and Isaac quickly bowed before making his greeting. Bradstock did the same, although Isaac did not miss the way that he continued to look towards Lady Sophia rather than smile amicably at all three ladies.

"I do hope that you have saved both dances for me, Lady Maria," Isaac asked, one hand pressed lightly to his heart as he rose from his bow. "I must pray you have not forgotten."

She laughed and lifted her wrist so that her dance card dangled from it.

"Indeed, I have not," she answered, pulling the silk ribbon from her wrist and handing it to him. "If you will note, Lord Ridlington, I have already taken the liberty of placing your name upon the two dances you specifically requested."

Fully aware of Bradstock's interest in this particular remark, Isaac turned to the side a little more so that Bradstock was no longer able to hear as well.

"Wonderful," he murmured, looking down at the dance card and seeing his name written on both the quadrille and the waltz. As he had feared, Lady Maria's dance card was already quite full and, had he not asked her to do as he had done, then he might very well have found himself without her company for the rest of the evening. "Thank you."

Bradstock asked Lady Sophia for her dance card and, of course, Isaac made certain to do so also, although he only placed his name down for one dance, taking the very last dance remaining. His eyes flicked over the card, seeing how Bradstock had written his name down in *two* spaces, just as Isaac had done with Lady Maria's dance card. There was certainly an interest in Lady Sophia from Bradstock, he noted, silently reminding himself to speak to his friend about the matter later that evening.

"Have you enjoyed the evening thus far?" Lady Hayward asked once the dance cards were returned to the ladies. "Have you had many conversations?"

Isaac shook his head.

"I am afraid that I have been very caught up in a discussion with Lord Penrith this evening, Lady Hayward, and have nothing of interest to speak of," he said, as Lady Maria dropped her gaze to the floor. "It was of no importance."

"Oh?"

Lady Sophia looked up at him, her eyes a little wide.

"I do hope that there is nothing wrong."

"No, no, indeed not," Isaac replied, with an impatient wave of his hand. "There are such things as Corn Laws, Lady Sophia which, in turn, have affected particular matters as regards both my own and Lord Penrith's estates. It does not help that both he and I have, it seems, suffered a very poor harvest indeed."

"I see."

Lady Sophia said nothing more, but when Isaac looked back at her, he saw that she was looking steadily back at Lady Maria, whose head was still a little bowed as though she found the conversation very dull indeed, but did not want to make it apparent for fear of being rude. His heart squeezed tightly for a moment, a little embarrassed that he had thought to even mention such a matter when there were ladies present. They would have no knowledge of such things and, therefore, very little interest in them. It was not a wise topic to continue mentioning.

"But that is not of any importance," he said, shrugging his shoulders. "Tell me, Lady Maria, have you had a pleasant day?"

Her head lifted at once.

"Indeed," she answered, although there was a tightness still playing about her mouth which she could not entirely hide from him. "Lady Sophia and I took a short trip to one or two shops this afternoon."

"Indeed!" he exclaimed, as Lady Sophia smiled happily. "And did you make any great purchases?"

Lady Maria's smile did not reach her eyes.

"A new silk ribbon," she answered, speaking a little more slowly than before, "and thereafter, two new books which I hope to read very soon."

Isaac nodded, thinking nothing of the fact that a young lady of quality might seek out a new novel or the like.

"Very good," he replied, as Lady Hayward watched on, saying nothing but watching her two charges carefully. "Might I enquire as to what their titles are?"

For some reason, this question seemed to bring an expression of panic to Lady Maria's face. Her eyes widened and her mouth opened just a fraction before she looked directly towards Lady Sophia, who gave a small shake of her head.

"I am afraid I do not recall," she answered, after a few moments. "It was certainly nothing of particular interest. Just one or two novels to keep me entertained in an evening."

He smiled, thinking quietly to himself that there was nothing at all that could interest him less than reading a novel or two.

"I do hope that you find them interesting, Lady Maria," he replied, as the first of the dances were called. "I am afraid that I have been much caught up in business matters today and have had very little time for joviality or the like."

Her smile was a little tight and certainly, there was no sparkle in her eyes. She turned her head away from him rather quickly and said something to Bradstock, leaving Isaac a little confused. Had he said something to upset her in some way?

"Do excuse me."

A deep voice from behind him made Isaac turn sharply, only to see a tall, thin gentleman looking directly at Lady Maria.

"I believe it is our dance, Lady Maria," he said, ignoring Isaac completely. "The cotillion."

The smile that came to Lady Maria's face lacked no warmth and, much to his surprise, Isaac felt a great kick of jealousy.

"But of course, Lord Venables," she replied, taking his proffered arm without any hesitation. "Do excuse me, please."

Isaac stepped back so that she could make her way past him without any difficulty, finding his gaze following her as she walked out to dance. His heart was making all manner of agitations within his chest and he felt the most ridiculous urge to go after her, to pull her from Lord Venables, and to dance with her himself.

You fool.

"Are you quite all right, Lord Ridlington?"

He turned back to Lady Hayward and placed a broad smile on his face – a smile which he did not truly feel.

"I am quite well," he replied, as Bradstock looked at

him curiously. "I – I was struggling to recall whether or not I am acquainted with Lord Venables, that is all."

Bradstock's lips twitched and he looked away, leaving Isaac to stammer awkwardly for a few minutes more. Eventually, however, Isaac was able to take his leave of Lady Hayward and excuse himself from her company entirely, his mind and heart so filled with swirling emotions and confusing thoughts that he felt as though he needed to step outside for a short time, simply so that he might find the space and the quietness he needed to understand all that he was feeling.

Shaking his head in the hope that it might settle his mind, Isaac reached out and took a glass of brandy from the nearby footman's tray. Taking a sip, he drew in a long breath and let it out again slowly, trying to calm all that now seemed to rage through him. Lady Maria would soon be on *his* arm, rather than that of Lord Venables and he would be the one to lead her out to dance. The waltz, being the most intimate of dances, would be solely for him and that, certainly, made Isaac feel a good deal better. Now a little more satisfied, Isaac threw back the rest of his brandy, before setting the empty glass down. There would be time to examine all that he felt at a later date. For the moment, he need only enjoy the evening as best he could and look forward to when *he* would be the one to take Lady Maria into his arms, when *he* would have her company entirely to himself.

The thought made a smile split across his face as his heart slammed hard against his chest. All he had to do now was wait.

CHAPTER NINE

M aria picked up her book and looked down at it
with a heavy heart. She had not told Lord
Ridlington the truth last evening and had felt her guilt
grow all the more as the lie had tripped from her tongue.
She had said that she could not recall the names of the
titles she had purchased when, of course, she was very
easily able to remember them. In addition, she had told
him that it had been nothing more than a couple of silly
novels, when the truth was that she had purchased two
books which would further her knowledge of the history
of England. She had always enjoyed reading about the
past, the kings and queens who had gone before, and the
exploits of those involved in the running of the country.
These two books in particular would increase her knowledge and understanding of past events, and Maria had
been very eager to begin reading.

"And then Lord Ridlington asked me about them,"
she murmured to herself, her jaw tightening as she closed
her eyes for a long moment. Lord Ridlington was

bringing up all manner of emotions in her heart and it was confusing her terribly. Even now, she could not bring herself to open the book and begin to read for, whenever she attempted to, she saw nothing but Lord Ridlington's smiling face and felt her heart twist with the heavy weight of guilt which now rested upon it.

She knew now that Lord Ridlington had intentions towards her. Over the last few weeks, his interest had become more and more apparent and, the day that he had asked her to accompany him for a walk in the park, Maria had felt her heart lift with delight. But now it was weighed down with more and more shame, more frustration, more pain. Whenever she saw or spoke to Lord Ridlington, she knew full well that she was not giving him a clear or true picture of the person she was. Whilst she had been determined enough to continue with her pretense, there had come an increasing awareness that Lord Ridlington did not know her for herself. And yet, Maria feared allowing him to know the truth of her heart, worried that he would step away from her entirely if she did so.

"But that would not matter," she said aloud, trying to convince herself with the words that she spoke. "There are many other gentlemen who might..."

Trailing off, Maria set the book back down on the table and sat down heavily in her chair near the fireplace. Putting her elbows on her knees, she pressed her hands over her eyes and let out a long sigh, fully aware that she was not being honest with herself.

"Lady Maria?"

She lifted her head at once, praying silently that her inward torment would not show on her features.

"Yes, Lady Hayward?"

The door opened and Lady Hayward stepped inside, smiling at her.

"Lady Maria, I am sorry to interrupt you this morning, when I know that you wish to rest, but I have some news for you which I thought could not wait."

"Oh?"

Maria made to rise to her feet but Lady Hayward waved her away, coming across the room quickly so that she might sit down in the chair opposite.

"I received a note from Lord Ridlington this morning," Lady Hayward continued, holding it out to Maria. "I thought you might like to read it."

For whatever reason, Maria's stomach dropped hard to the floor as she looked at the note held in Lady Hayward's outstretched hand. Her tongue seemed to swell, and prevent her from speaking as Lady Hayward waited expectantly, and her heart was clamoring within her as she attempted to reach out to take it.

"Lady Maria?" Lady Hayward's voice held puzzlement. "Are you quite all right?"

Struggling to find the words to say, never mind the strength to say it, Maria managed nothing more than a shake of her head, although her gaze remained fixed on the note.

"Then mayhap I shall simply express the sentiments contained within," Lady Hayward replied, as Maria nodded, closing her eyes for a moment or two in an attempt to regain her composure.

She felt sure that she knew what was contained within the note and, whilst part of her was thrilled with Lord Ridlington's interest, there was another part of her that dreaded hearing his sentiments, knowing that they came from nothing more than believing a falsehood.

"He states, very eloquently, that he thinks very highly of you, Lady Maria," Lady Hayward began, her expression gentle but her eyes sharp as she continued to glance down now at the unfolded note. "He asks my permission to court you, or states that, if required, he will write to your father to ask the very same." She tilted her head to the right, studying Maria carefully as Maria herself opened her eyes and slowly dragged in air. "There is also mention of the fact that he believes you to be quite amiable and, indeed, open to such a thing, Lady Maria."

A ghost of a smile whispered across Maria's face.

"Of course I am," she said, without hesitation. "To be courted is...."

Lady Hayward frowned, folding up the note again and reaching across to set it on the table where Maria's books were.

"And yet, if you do not wish to accept him, then I will neither encourage nor force you," she said, gently, as Maria felt tears begin to burn in the corner of her eyes. "I know that I have said it many times, but I shall say it again now, Lady Maria: to find oneself wed to a gentleman whom you care nothing for is not a wise choice. If Lord Ridlington does not –"

"He does!"

Maria's startled interjection surprised her just as much as Lady Hayward who, for a moment, said nothing but blinked rather rapidly in surprise. Maria felt herself crumple inwardly, covering her face with her hands and making Lady Hayward exclaim at once, coming forward to settle a hand on Maria's shoulder.

"Lady Maria?" she asked, as Maria continued to hide her face from Lady Hayward, her heart crying out with both pain and confusion. "Are you troubled about something?"

Forcing her tears back, Maria dropped her hands and looked up into Lady Hayward's face.

"I have found myself a little confused over Lord Ridlington," she admitted, softly. "These last two weeks, since I have been spending more time in his company, I have found him very amiable indeed. He is handsome, well-spoken, and seemingly kindhearted, and the way that I have found myself feeling has been..."

She shook her head, unable to find the words to express the truth of how she felt.

"I quite understand," Lady Hayward replied, softly. "But that is no cause for confusion and upset, Lady Maria, surely? If you have such an affection for Lord Ridlington, then there is nothing that you need be concerned about. And, if you do not, or if for some other reason, you decide against him, I can assure you that there are many other gentlemen who will seek to court you." She smiled at Maria but Maria could not bring herself to return it, such was the heaviness in her heart. "Have you not noticed just how many gentlemen have been eager for your company this last fortnight? You have never been lacking company for dances, you have always had excellent conversation, and there have been gentlemen calling upon you almost every day!" Lady Hayward patted Maria's hand and then rose to sit back in her chair. "You will have plenty of choice, Lady Maria, I am quite certain."

Maria knew that her tears were imminent and did nothing to stop them, pulling the handkerchief from her sleeve and dabbing at her eyes. Lady Hayward's smile faded in an instant and she made to hurry towards Maria once more, but Maria held out one hand and shook her head.

"I must be honest with you, Lady Hayward," she said, brokenly. "The only reason I believe that more gentlemen are interested in me this Season is because I have changed my character somewhat."

Lady Hayward frowned.

"What do you mean?"

"Indeed, it is all the worse for Lord Ridlington because I have pulled him into my farce all the more!" Maria exclaimed, not answering Lady Hayward's question. "I thought that, should he ask to court me, I would find a way to express the truth of my character but, instead, I now find myself completely and utterly confused. I am lost and broken and uncertain and – and, I believe, beginning to feel more for Lord Ridlington than I ever expected." Her eyes closed tightly as rivers of tears flowed down her cheeks, forcing her to press her handkerchief to them one at a time. Sniffing indelicately, she shook her head and drew in a ragged breath. "You will think very poorly of me, Lady Hayward, but I could not *bear* another Season where not even a single gentleman thought to call upon me! I know that father is anxious for me to wed and therefore, I realized that I needed to change what was presented to the *ton*."

Lady Hayward held up one hand, palm out towards Maria.

"Pray, wait a moment, Lady Maria," she said, speaking with infinite gentleness. "I do not understand what you mean."

The words began to tumble out of Maria one after the other, as though she was entirely unable to keep the truth from spilling from her heart.

"I overheard my father speaking to you, Lady Hayward," she said, wretchedly. "I did not listen for long, I confess, but certainly it was long enough to realize that my father is afraid I shall never wed. Therefore, I had a great burden upon my heart when I returned to London with you."

Lady Hayward's expression softened, sympathy filling her expression.

"Lady Maria, I am quite sure that you *will* find a suitable match in time," she said, as Maria continued to dab at her eyes with the handkerchief. "To allow yourself to become held back by fear will only place a heavy weight upon your shoulders. One that does not need to be there."

Shaking her head, Maria sniffed twice and then tried to continue.

"I began to consider my conduct last Season, and during the winter months," she said, her voice hoarse and rasping. "You may be aware – in fact, I am sure that you know that I am inclined towards reading and learning as much as I can. Whilst my father has never expressly forbidden me from doing so, I know that he has always been a little concerned about my interests."

"Interests which I reassured him were to be encouraged," Lady Hayward replied, as though she was afraid that Maria would think that she had agreed with the Duke. "I do not think that there is anything wrong in being learned, Lady Maria."

A small, sad smile pulled at Maria's lips.

"But the *beau monde* look upon a lady of knowledge with great disdain, do they not?" she asked, her voice rasping now. "I realized, as I reflected on what had taken place last Season, that every time I joined a conversation, every time I spoke about what I had been reading or thinking of, most of those present would either look away or turn away completely. I did not realize the truth of it before now."

Lady Hayward had begun to frown, her blue eyes now sharp and fixed.

"You mean to say that you believe there was no particular interest from the gentlemen of the *ton* simply because you expressed an interest in what they spoke of? In matters that you also have a full awareness and understanding about?"

"Indeed," Maria replied, heavily. "So, this Season, I deliberately chose to remain silent when, previously, I would have asked questions or shared what I thought. There have been times when I have been forced to bite my tongue to keep from speaking! I have done all I can to hide the fact that I am a bluestocking and, in doing so, have seen many more gentleman eager to be in my company." Her head dropped low and she closed her eyes, her heart so heavy with guilt and shame that it felt as though it were being slowly torn apart. "And what is worse, I have had Lady Sophia assisting me. She has played the pianoforte on my behalf, whilst I have pretended to do so. The drawing I showed to Lord Ridlington was not my own, but that of Lady Sophia. The desire to present myself as an eligible young lady of the *ton,* who is practically perfect in her behavior, her manner and her interests has grown so great that it has practically overwhelmed me. Lady Sophia has been so very kind but, in addition, she has also attempted to warn me about such a deception. She has asked me to consider what I am doing, has asked me repeatedly whether or not I wish to continue with such a charade, but I confess, Lady Hayward, that I have been quite determined." She did not dare look up at the lady for fear that what she would see on her face would be all the more damning. "And now that Lord Ridlington has asked to court me, I am afraid that he is only doing so because he believes me to be someone I am not! What is worse is that my heart *does* hold an affection for him – an affection which I have not been able to quash – and now I am so very lost in confusion and doubt that I do not know what to do!"

These last words came out in a rush as Maria's tears began to fall once more, her heart aching so dreadfully that it was all she could do to contain herself. She had thought she might feel a little better for having spoken so honestly to Lady Hayward but instead, there was nothing but a gaping hole where her heart should be. She felt as though she were covered in shame, torn down with guilt and left cowering in the face of the consequences which would, she was certain, now be brought to bear.

"My dear Lady Maria." Maria's head lifted in surprise at hearing the kindness in Lady Hayward's voice. "What torment you must have endured!"

Lady Hayward rose and came towards Maria again, reaching out both hands to her. When Maria came to stand, Lady Hayward said nothing more but simply embraced her, holding her close like a mother would do. Maria felt herself begin to break all over again, tears forming in the corners of her eyes and sobs racking her frame. And all the while, Lady Hayward said nothing but simply held her tightly, allowing all of the pain and the guilt to wash through Maria's heart until it felt as though she had nothing left.

"Now," Lady Hayward murmured, stepping back but reaching to keep hold of Maria's hands. "I will first inform you that what you have chosen to do is not, of course, the right path. Deception is never wise, Lady Maria, but I shall not remain on the subject any further, for I can see that you are already greatly distraught as a result of what you have done." She smiled softly at Maria, who closed her eyes and dropped her head. "There is pain in your heart, is there not?" Lady Hayward continued, as Maria nodded. "Pain that has come from so many things. From the fear that your father will be proven to be correct, from the realization that the *beau monde* do not always think well of ladies who know more than they ought, and now from the realization that you have come to care for Lord Ridlington, without him fully being aware of who you are." She squeezed Maria's hands. "I can understand that there is an eagerness within your heart to accept Lord Ridlington's request to court you," she continued, softly, "but at the same time, a great burden pulls away your happiness and delight. Is that not so?"

Maria nodded, her throat aching with the effort of keeping her tears contained.

"It is," she whispered, still not quite able to look at her chaperone. "Lady Hayward, I thought I was doing the right thing. I was so very glad to see the interest which was soon directed towards me for, to have gentlemen seeking me out, eager for my company and the like, has thrown such a sense of astonishment and delight over me that I became determined to continue with my façade." She shook her head. "There have been times when I have been almost desperate to speak of what I know, of what I understand and to further converse about the matter with others. But in remaining silent, I have gained the interest of the *beau monde*."

"And has it been worth it?" Lady Hayward asked, gently. "Have you found yourself glad now that you have done so?"

Maria shook her head, knowing now that the pain and sorrow which overwhelmed her spirits was much greater than that which she had felt before.

"I believe Lord Ridlington has a great consideration for you, Lady Maria," Lady Hayward continued, quietly. "But if you are to accept his court, then you must speak to him of the truth. You must tell him about the pianoforte, the drawing, and the fact that you are both well-read and eager to read more. I can assure you that it will be for the best."

"But what if he does not have any desire to court me any longer?" Maria asked, a sense of desperation rising up within her. "What am I to do then?"

Lady Hayward opened her mouth to answer, then closed it again and gave Maria a small shrug.

"I think that is a question best answered once you know of Lord Ridlington's reaction to what you have to say," she replied, after a few moments. "There can be no definite answer at present. Do you believe you have the strength to tell Lord Ridlington the truth, Lady Maria?"

It was a question which Maria felt was flung at her, leaving her examining her own heart and her own strength, wondering whether or not she would be able to speak as openly to Lord Ridlington as she had done here.

"I must be honest with him," she whispered, knowing that there was no other response but this. "I cannot continue to pretend."

"No," Lady Hayward agreed. "You cannot. It would not be wise, Lady Maria, not when there is so much at stake." She smiled gently and Maria shook her head again, certainly feeling a little more settled but yet aware that there would be great difficulty to come. "Might I suggest," Lady Hayward said, getting to her feet and settling one hand gently on Maria's shoulder, "that, when you *do* have a few moments to speak to the gentleman, you begin by telling him of what you feel?"

Maria looked up sharply, her breath catching in her throat.

"I do not think that I can do such a thing."

"It would be wise," Lady Hayward replied, kindly. "It is because of what you feel that you have the urge to speak the truth to him, to tell him that you are, in fact, something of a bluestocking and that there is no shame in your heart because of it. He must know *why* you are determined to tell him such a thing and if you speak of your heart, then that will surely be of great importance to him."

Maria dropped her head and let out a long, slow breath.

"I – I will consider what I have to say," she answered, not wishing to agree to any specific course of action as yet. "I cannot thank you enough, Lady Hayward, for your understanding and your advice." She looked up at her again, her vision a little blurred by yet more tears. "It is more than I expected and certainly more than I deserve."

Lady Hayward smiled and pressed Maria's shoulder once more.

"I am only glad that you were able to tell me," she answered. "Rest now, Lady Maria. I will have a tea tray sent to you."

Maria nodded, waiting until the door had closed behind Lady Hayward before she let the full thrust of her emotions crash through her. With tears pouring down her cheeks, she leaned forward and pressed her handkerchief to her eyes, as fresh sobs racked her frame. This had all been a mistake. She had believed she was doing the right thing, and had been glad to see the effects of her supposed change, but in doing so she had managed to encourage Lord Ridlington to believe a lie – and believe it, he had. To know now that he had an interest in her, an interest in the person he believed her to be, tore terribly at her heart.

"I will tell you everything," she promised, as though he were standing in the room with her. "And whatever you choose to do, I shall accept it without question."

CHAPTER TEN

"Thank you."

Isaac took the note from his butler and opened it at once, all the more intrigued as to what it might say. Ever since he had written to Lady Hayward, his thoughts had been running in all directions. He had no certainty as to what reply he would receive, but the hope that filled his heart simply would not leave him. He was doing all he could to tell himself that this was akin to a matter of business and that, should he receive a rebuttal, it would mean very little for him to simply go in search of another young lady in Lady Maria's place.

The problem was that his heart did not believe it.

"'Thank you for your letter, Lord Ridlington,'" he read aloud. "'In fairness to Lady Maria, I have spoken to her of your intentions and your request and have given her some time to think on it. I believe that she wishes to speak to you herself and will do so very soon.'"

A frown knotted his brows together as he sat back in

his chair, not quite certain what such a response could mean. Did Lady Maria want to speak to him because she intended to refuse and wanted to express her reasons for doing so? He could not think of any other reason for her to wish to talk to him privately. Rubbing the line that had formed between his brows, he made to get up in to go in search of a brandy, only for there to come a knock at the door.

Is there another note?

"Yes?"

The butler stepped inside.

"My lord, Lord Bradstock has arrived."

"Oh." Having not expected his friend, Isaac chose to remain where he was. "Of course. From now on, simply show any of my acquaintances in. I shall always be glad to see them." Given that his acquaintances numbered very few, Isaac did not think that he would often have afternoon callers and, if he did, most likely it would be Bradstock.

The butler nodded and disappeared again, only for Bradstock to step inside a moment or two later, the usual wide grin settled on his face. After enquiring as to whether or not he might fetch something more for either Isaac or Lord Bradstock, the butler withdrew and closed the door behind him.

"Do sit down," Isaac murmured, as Bradstock flopped back into a comfortable chair, tilted his head and grinned at Isaac.

"I hear that you have been taking a particular interest in one Lady Maria," he said, tilting his head to one side. "That is what the *ton* is saying, certainly!"

Isaac grimaced.

"I care nothing for what the *ton* think," he replied, as Bradstock chuckled. "And you know very well that I am considering Lady Maria."

Bradstock nodded and then pushed himself out of his chair with a seemingly great effort. Isaac watched him as he meandered across the room to the small table at the back, where the brandy and whisky were kept.

"Has she fulfilled all of your requirements?" Bradstock asked as Isaac grunted, not wanting to discuss the matter with Bradstock in any particular detail. "You have not found her lacking?"

"No, I have not," Isaac replied, firmly. "As far as I can tell, she appears to be quite perfect."

Bradstock poured himself a generous measure of brandy before tilting the decanter in Isaac's direction, who nodded in response. Returning to his chair, Bradstock handed one glass to Isaac before he resumed his seat. His eyes were a little thoughtful and, much to Isaac's relief, the grin that had been plastered across Bradstock's face was now quite gone.

"I think I have intentions towards Lady Sophia," he said, as Isaac blinked rapidly, trying to hide his surprise. "She is quite lovely."

"Intentions?" Isaac repeated, utterly astonished to hear such a thing from Bradstock. "You have never had any particular intentions towards anyone, Bradstock. You told me so yourself!"

Bradstock smiled, but it was not a smile of mirth or mischievousness as Isaac had expected. Instead, it spoke of a gentle consideration towards Lady Sophia which Isaac had never seen before.

"I – I had known that you found Lady Sophia a little fascinating, certainly," he continued, as Bradstock lifted one shoulder in a half shrug. "I had meant to speak to you about her, for I thought it nothing more than a passing interest which would quickly fade."

"And you feared that I might behave a little inappropriately towards her, given that she is only newly out?" Bradstock replied, with a lift of his eyebrow. "I confess that, at first, I thought that a mere flirtation might satisfy me, but the more time I have spent in her company, the more I have come to realize that I hold a deep and unrelenting interest in the lady which I simply cannot remove." He shook his head, a small frown catching his brow for a moment. "No, it is more than that. It is more than just a mere interest. There is an intimacy between us now which will never be forgotten. I find that I want to build on such an intimacy so that this... this *affection* which is within my heart grows into something all the more wonderful." His eyes were blazing with determination, his hands spread wide as he gestured. "Lady Sophia is the very best of young ladies, as far as I am concerned. I can do nothing but fall at her feet and pray that she will accept me."

The way that Bradstock spoke made Isaac wince inwardly. He was so very free with his expressions of affection for Lady Sophia whilst Isaac himself battled to even permit himself to acknowledge what was going on within his own heart. Part of him wished that he had the very same freedom as Bradstock, desperate to be able to speak of what he struggled with at present, but yet finding that there was something within him that held him back. He had not the passion nor the zeal that Bradstock expressed but, somehow, he knew that if he only permitted himself to let all that he felt free from within his heart, he might then find the very same.

"You – you look troubled."

Catching himself, Isaac looked back at Bradstock and saw the worry in his eyes.

"No, indeed, it is not that I have any qualms or concerns when it comes to yourself and Lady Sophia," he said, quickly. "Pray, forgive me. It is only that I...." His eyes strayed to the note which was settled on the table next to him. "I have written to Lady Hayward to seek her permission to court Lady Maria."

Bradstock said nothing, although there was not even a single flicker of surprise in his expression.

"She has replied to me – Lady Hayward, that is – and has stated that Lady Maria wishes to speak to me about my intentions," he continued, rubbing his chin thoughtfully. "I cannot help but wonder what she wishes to say."

"Then go and call upon her and ask," Bradstock replied, with a tired wave of his hand. "Goodness, Ridlington. You are one of the most confused gentlemen I believe I have ever met!"

Feeling a trifle insulted, Isaac chose to take a sip of his brandy before he gave a response, seeing the weariness in Bradstock's expression and wondering at it.

"I do not think I am confused," he replied, only for Bradstock to throw back his head and laugh. The sound was grating and hard, making Isaac's anger begin to stir.

"You are *very* confused, Ridlington," came the quick response. "You have this long list of specific expectations that must be fulfilled in their entirety before you will be satisfied with the lady. And yet, when faced with the fact that you might now actually *care* for someone, you choose to disregard that and fix your gaze solely upon your record of requirements. But try as you might, you cannot truly hide the great weight of emotion which settles over your heart, and thus, you find yourself greatly confused. You try to think of your requirements, try to tell yourself that Lady Maria is quite perfect in every way thus far, perhaps praying that there will be nothing which spoils her thus far unstained record as you begin courtship whilst if you were truly honest with yourself, you would see that she is more than enough for you already."

Isaac swallowed hard, knowing full well that Bradstock was absolutely correct in all that he said, but refusing to let himself acknowledge it aloud.

"I – I have my reasons for my particular standards," he said, in what was a poor attempt at defending himself. "I believe that, in holding to them, I will find the perfect match and therefore will have a long and satisfactory marriage."

"Satisfactory?" Bradstock stared at Isaac as though he was being utterly ridiculous. "That is all you think of? You want your marriage to be one which is continually measured and considered?"

Isaac nodded.

"I do. And if there is something which is causing difficulty, then I would expect the matter to be resolved very quickly. But if I choose a bride who fulfills all that I expect, then such instances will be very rare indeed."

Bradstock ran one hand down his face and groaned aloud. "You are utterly mistaken, Ridlington," he said, his words firm and direct. "That is not what will make a satisfactory marriage. It will make for an extremely difficult one."

Isaac stiffened.

"I cannot see how –"

"Lady Maria does *not* fulfill all of your requirements, I am certain of it," Bradstock interrupted. "One way or another, you will find that she is not the perfect young lady that you have imagined. I do not speak of anything specific but rather the knowledge that a young lady of quality might very well hide a great deal in order to be presentable and appear as eligible as possible." He shook his head and picked up his brandy glass. "But regardless of that, if you truly believe that finding the supposedly perfect young lady according to your requirements will ensure that she will make you the most wonderful wife who will very rarely cause any 'difficulties', as you call them, then you are sadly mistaken."

A wave of embarrassment crashed over Isaac and he felt his anger flare hotter again but, with an effort, contained himself.

"I heard it from my own father," he said hotly, lifting his chin and glaring at Bradstock. "As a child, I grew up in a household of continual strife, simply because my father chose poorly when it came to his bride. He married the lady he believed he cared for, only for it to turn out very poorly. And once you are wed, there is nothing that can be done!"

Bradstock shook his head sorrowfully.

"That may be so, Ridlington, but that does not mean that your marriage will be the same," he said quietly. "It may have been that your mother accepted the marriage but had no feelings whatsoever for your father. Perhaps your father *was* hasty. But such things do not matter when it comes to your own heart." He leaned forward in his chair, fixing Isaac with his gaze. "Lady Sophia, I know, has a heart very similar to my own. We share an affection. I intend to court her and then to propose to her, thereby making certain of my intentions and making certain that she shares them." His lips flattened for a moment as though he was struggling to know what to say to express himself well. "And when I ask her to wed me, as I fully intend to do, change will come into my life and into my home. I will not expect everything to remain as it is at present. Rather, I hope that I will continue to develop my knowledge of her."

Isaac twisted his lips but Bradstock held up one hand and went on.

"I do not mean in that sense, but rather that my *acquaintance* of her will continue to grow. I want to know what she thinks, what she feels, what troubles her, and the like. I wish to share my own heart with her in return. There should be a trust formed between us which will not only permit her but *encourage* her, to speak openly to me, knowing that I will do all that I can to support her in whatever she wishes. I will not berate her for any 'difficulties' which might be caused, for I might be the one to cause them! Our marriage is not to simply be a satisfactory arrangement, but will instead be one of respect and, I hope, of love." He shook his head again, rose to his feet, and threw back the rest of his brandy in one gulp. "I feel a great deal of sorrow for you, that you are deliberately choosing not to experience that, Ridlington."

Isaac did not know what to say. Bradstock had somehow managed to place his finger directly on all that he had been struggling with inwardly, things which he had never once shared with another person. There was no anger left him now, only a sorrowful awareness that his friend had spoken the truth. A truth which he had not wanted to acknowledge for a long time.

"I will take my leave," Bradstock said, as Isaac looked up at him, seeing no anger in his friend's eyes but rather a quiet understanding. "I do not leave as an enemy but still as your friend. I only pray that something of what I have said will be of benefit to you, Ridlington. It is, I believe, for your best."

Isaac closed his eyes and heard the door close gently behind Bradstock. For the first time, he began to question everything he had ever clung to, recalling what his father had said and pushing it to one side to be replaced by what Bradstock had just told him. Was it possible to have a marriage that shared both affection and understanding? Could such a marriage bring happiness, rather than strife? His mind did not want to believe it, his heart quailing like a trapped bird that is terrified of its cage. To break free of it would be to allow himself to believe something entirely different, to trust that to let his heart free of all that he felt would bring a newfound happiness.

He groaned aloud, sitting forward and plowing his hands through his hair. How could he speak to Lady Maria when his own heart and mind were in such turmoil? How could he express all that was now bearing down upon him when he did not know what to do next?

His list of requirements seemed to pull themselves apart before his very eyes, ripping and shredding themselves into tiny pieces which disintegrated completely. Was he willing to let them go? Was he ready to simply step forward without any real expectations?

"No," he breathed, closing his eyes tightly his fingers gripping together as he fought for some sort of resolve. "I cannot. Not yet."

A vision of Lady Maria floated in front of his eyes and Isaac let out another loud groan. He had always prided himself on being level headed, on being well thought out and considered in all that he did, but now it seemed as though everything was closing in on him.

"My Lord?"

He looked up, astonished to see none other than Lady Maria standing in the doorway, with Lady Hayward just behind her.

"I do apologize for intruding," she said, taking a small step forward as doubt flashed across her expression. "Your butler said —"

"No."

Isaac rose to his feet, slicing the air with his hands.

"No, I cannot see you at the moment, Lady Maria. I cannot!"

She stared at him, wide-eyed as the color drained from her face.

"I do not wish to speak to you at this present moment, Lady Maria!" Isaac exclaimed, knowing that he spoke with great rudeness, but finding himself so overwhelmed and confused that he could say nothing else. "Lord Bradstock has only just taken his leave and what he has said to me..."

He groaned again and rubbed one hand across his forehead, his eyes squeezing shut.

"Lord... Lord Bradstock?"

Lady Maria's voice was soft, filled with a fear that he had never heard before.

"Come, Lady Maria." Lady Hayward put a hand on Lady Maria's arm, pulling her gently away. "We should take our leave."

"What has he said?" Lady Maria asked as Isaac opened his eyes to see her shaking off Lady Hayward's restraining hand. "Has he realized the truth?"

Isaac blinked in confusion, his head beginning to throb painfully.

"The truth?" he stated, his stomach churning furiously. "Lord Bradstock has spoken a good many truths to me this afternoon, Lady Maria, and now I must consider them. I must consider *all* of them."

"I did not mean to deceive you!" she cried, as Isaac looked up at her sharply. "It is only –"

"Deceive?" His voice rang out across the room, just as Lady Maria gasped and flung one hand over her mouth. "You have deceived me?"

Lady Maria shook her head wordlessly, although it was not clear now whether or not she was attempting to deny what she had said or simply refusing to answer him.

Lady Hayward stepped forward. Her eyes were narrowed and angry, as a spot of color appeared on each cheek.

"I think you have said enough, Lord Ridlington," she stated, her voice cold and hard. "To dismiss Lady Maria in such a way when, only earlier today, you wrote to ask if you might court her is... is utterly despicable." She took a small step towards him, leaving Lady Maria to stand in the doorway, tears now spilling from her cheeks. "There is much that Lady Maria needs to explain, but I will *not* permit her to do so now, not when you have spoken to her in such a manner."

Isaac's jaw worked furiously, feeling both over-whelming shame at the tears in Lady Maria's eyes and a great sense of fury at what she had said.

"But to deceive me?"

"It is not in the way that you might think, Lord Ridlington," Lady Hayward stated, furiously. "It was not cruelly meant nor in any way meant to injure you. But as I have said, I will not allow her to speak of it now. Perhaps once you have calmed yourself and find yourself in a state where you are not only willing to listen but to speak respectfully, we might attempt to sit down together. Until then, good day!"

And so saying, she turned on her heel and marched back towards the door, taking Lady Maria with her. The door closed tightly behind them, leaving Isaac to stare after them both, finding himself all the more perplexed at what had been said – and what had been left unsaid.

Utterly despicable.

The anger which had coursed through him seemed to

fade away like the retreating tide. Now that he was left alone, Isaac found himself sinking back down into his chair, his heavy breaths the only sound. A tumult of emotions swamped him and he closed his eyes tightly, leaning his head back against the chair as he attempted to calm his frantically beating heart.

Just what had he done?

CHAPTER ELEVEN

"You do not have to attend this evening, Maria."

"I am aware of that," Maria replied, as Lady Hayward reached out to put one hand over hers. "But what good is remaining at the townhouse? I will only lose heart all the more and end up lingering in despondency and despair."

Lady Hayward searched her face for another moment before nodding and reaching up to rap on the roof of the carriage. There was no turning back now. Maria had made her decision.

"I am so very sorry to hear of what occurred, Lady Maria," Lady Sophia said quietly, as the carriage began to pull away. "I did not ever think that Lord Ridlington would behave in such a manner."

"He was very troubled," Maria replied, fixing her gaze out of the window rather than attempting to make out Lady Sophia's features in the gloom. "I am uncertain as to what troubled him so but, needless to say, my words did not aid him in any way. Rather, I am quite certain that I made his struggle a good deal worse."

She closed her eyes and tried not to let the memory of what she had said and how he had reacted pull at her heart, but still, it returned to her mind. She could see him standing here, slicing the air with his hand as he told her to leave him, told her outright that he did not want to speak with her at that moment. Her heart had been filled with a terrible fear, a fear which had forced her to speak – and speak, she had. To talk of deception had been unwise, for the shock and the confusion of what she had said had filled his features and he had grown all the more agitated. She had thought that Lord Bradstock had, somehow, come to realize that she was not all that she seemed and that, in attempting to protect his friend, he had gone to tell him what he had learned. Too late, she had realized that Lord Ridlington spoke of something else, too late did she see that it was nothing whatsoever to do with her. The words she had spoken could not be taken back, however. They lingered on, both in her heart and in Lord Ridlington's mind.

"Regardless, Lady Maria, he did not speak to you in a manner which was at all appropriate," Lady Hayward said, a trace of anger still lingering in her voice. "You had gone to speak to him of what was in your heart and from the very moment that you stepped inside, he was dismissive, cold, and utterly disrespectful."

"It is not as though I spoke well either, however," Maria replied, grateful for Lady Hayward's protection of her but still fully aware that what she had said had made things all the worse. "If I had been more guarded if I had merely taken a moment before speaking, then Lord Ridlington might well have been much calmer."

"That may be so," Lady Hayward agreed, "but bear in mind that he was dismissive of you *before* you spoke, Lady Maria, as well as being utterly reprehensible thereafter. I am glad that I removed you from his company, for it was clear to me that he could not, for whatever reason, be civil." Her eyes flashed as the carriage began to slow as it made its way through some of the winding London streets. "I do hope, however, that in time, both you and he will be able to discuss things in a reasonable and calm manner. Whatever was troubling him was clearly of great importance, and what troubles you is of equal significance."

A small sigh escaped Lady Hayward's lips and a deep guilt once more threw itself over Maria. Had she decided simply to continue as she had done before, had she eschewed any thought of a pretense, then she might now be making her way to the ball without any difficulties or struggle tied around her heart. She might have been perfectly content, instead of – as she was now – battling to keep her thoughts in order, to keep her mind from losing itself completely to despair. She would have felt none of this shame, none of this guilt which continually tore at her spirit – and, of course, she might very well also have felt nothing whatsoever towards Lord Ridlington.

That was the very worst of things, Maria thought to herself, her head dropping low for a moment as pain began to burn through her. Regardless of what occurred between herself and Lord Ridlington, she still found herself thinking of him often. There was still that gentle affection there, that longing to be more to him than a mere acquaintance. To have acknowledged that, to have allowed herself to realize that she was drawn to him in a manner which seemed to capture her whole being, had not brought any sort of delight with it. Rather, it was a painful, agonizing realization, for with it had come the knowledge that she had to tell him the truth. She had to speak to him of her deception, of her shame, and pray that he would, somehow, understand – and, if he did not, if he chose to turn his back on her, to reject her utterly, then whilst Maria had silently promised herself to accept it, she had found that even the thought of him doing so had brought her nothing but pain.

Now, it seemed quite inevitable that he would do as she feared, that he would tell her there could be no continuation of their acquaintance any longer. Her heart seemed to shrink within her chest as the carriage came to a stop outside Lord and Lady Winthrop's townhouse. This evening's ball would bring her no delight, no plea-sure, no joy. Instead, she would have to play a part, fixing a smile on her face and expressing delight to whomever she danced with.

But I am very adept at doing so, am I not? she asked herself, wincing as she prepared to step out of the carriage. Lady Hayward was waiting for her, giving her a long, searching look before she smiled, turned, and began to make her way up the steps towards the front of the house, leaving Maria to follow. Maria took in a deep breath, lifting her chin and setting her shoulders, attempting to find some sort of strength, some sort of courage which would help her to endure the rest of this evening with dignity and poise.

He will not be present, she told herself, as she climbed each and every step. *You will not see him here. There is nothing to fear in that regard.*

Which was why, as she stepped inside the townhouse, her heart turned over in horror as she discovered that the very gentleman she had believed would be absent this evening was standing in the hallway, only a few steps away from her.

Her breath hitched and for a moment, she did not know where to look. She stood stock-still, one hand at her heart, unable to lift her gaze from him. He was not looking at her and did not seem to be aware of her presence thus far.

"Come, Lady Maria."

A hand touched her arm and Maria jumped visibly, turning to see Lady Hayward looking at her with a gentle compassion in her eyes.

"Even if he is present, you need not give him all of your attention," the lady remarked, keeping her voice low so that they would not be overheard. "We should greet our hosts and then enter the ballroom without delay. If he wishes to speak to you, my dear, he will come in search of you." She smiled and dropped her hand. "Come."

Maria managed a small nod and found herself following Lady Hayward on legs which trembled and shook, forcing herself not to turn her head and look at Lord Ridlington, but instead fixing her attention solely on their hosts. She was certain that Lord Ridlington would notice her presence at some point, would be aware of her entering the ballroom, but she dared not turn back to look at him. She had to believe that, just as Lady Hayward had said, if he wished to speak to her, then he would.

"Good evening, Lord and Lady Winthrop." Dropping into a curtsey, Maria spoke quietly to their hosts for a few moments, thanking them for their invitation and the like, before being directed towards the ballroom. Lady Sophia came after her and, together, the three ladies made their way into the room, with Maria's stomach still churning furiously, and every single part of her feeling tense and taut.

"Lord Ridlington has not yet come into the ballroom," she heard Lady Sophia remark, as they surveyed the scene before them. "I looked before we stepped inside. For whatever reason, he lingers in the hallway."

Maria's lips curved sadly as she remembered the very first time that she had set eyes on Lord Ridlington. He had been doing the same thing that evening as he was this evening, remaining quietly in the hallway rather than joining the rest of the guests in the ballroom. She remembered just how her curiosity had grown as she had watched him and the embarrassment which had filled her as he had looked back at her and seen her watching him. How much had changed since then!

"Good evening, Lady Sophia, Lady Hayward, Lady Maria!"

Her thoughts were torn from her as Lord Bradstock came to join them, his eyes lingering on Lady Sophia for a long moment before he bowed.

"Good evening," Maria murmured, her heart beginning to quicken in her chest as questions began to fill her mind with respect to what he had said to Lord Ridlington, just before she had arrived at Lord Ridlington's home, for that shocking encounter. She pressed her lips together tightly, preventing herself from speaking any of those questions aloud, knowing that she could not simply bombard Lord Bradstock in such a manner when he had only just joined their company.

"I do hope that we might dance together this evening, Lady Sophia?" Lord Bradstock's interest was directed solely towards Lady Sophia, and Maria felt no insult nor irritation whatsoever. Instead, she found herself to be quite glad that a gentleman such as Lord Bradstock was showing such an inclination towards Lady Sophia, as she had come to think very highly of the man indeed and was quite certain, therefore, that he would suit Lady Sophia very well indeed. One glance at Lady Hayward told her that she also was glad of Lord Bradstock's interest, for there was a small smile lingering on Lady Hayward's face as she watched her daughter hand Lord Bradstock her dance card. Perhaps there *would* be a betrothal this Season after all.

Just not my own betrothal.

"Lady Maria?"

Lord Bradstock smiled at her and held out one hand. It took a moment for Maria to realize what he was asking for, and another moment to pull her dance card from her wrist and hand it to him.

"Lord Ridlington is present this evening," he said, looking at her with a small smile before dropping his gaze back to her dance card. "I am sure that he will be eager to dance with you."

"Without wishing to be contradictory, Lord Brad-stock, I do not think that he will be," Maria replied, before she could stop herself. "I was dismissed from his presence only yesterday."

Lord Bradstock, who had been about to hand her back her dance card, froze in place, one hand holding out her dance card whilst his eyes widened with evident shock.

"I believe we called upon him shortly after your departure," Maria continued, despite the warning glances which came from both Lady Sophia and Lady Hayward. "He appeared to be in a state of great distress which, I am afraid to say, I only added to."

Lord Bradstock closed his eyes tightly for a moment, then shook his head.

"I am very sorry indeed, Lady Maria," he said, quietly. "I believe that I may well be responsible for his fit of temper and I am deeply sorry to hear that you were dismissed in what must have been a very rude manner indeed."

He sighed heavily, running one hand over his eyes as Maria watched him carefully.

"Might I ask, Lord Bradstock," she said, knowing that what she was about to ask was a little presumptuous, "what it was that you spoke of? He appeared to be angry with me for some reason and I feared that...."

She trailed off, unable to express the truth to Lord Bradstock.

"I did speak of you," Lord Bradstock replied, looking back at her steadily, "but it was not in a rude, conde-scending, or improper manner. Rather, I–" He broke off, frowning hard as his gaze drifted away. Maria did not say a single word as she waited, praying that both Lady Hayward and Lady Sophia would do the same. There was clearly something on Lord Bradstock's mind, and he appeared to be considering whether or not he would speak of it. "Lady Maria," he said, speaking with great gravitas in both his expression and his voice, as his brows lowered over his eyes and his lips thinned. "Lord Ridlington cares for you." Maria pressed one hand to her heart, feeling it leap wildly in her chest. "But he refuses to permit himself to accept it," Lord Ridlington continued, waving a hand in frustration. "He has a list of requirements that any young lady of his acquaintance must meet before he can even *consider* them and thus –"

"Requirements?" Lady Hayward's voice was sharp, cutting through Lord Bradstock's words and speaking the very question which had settled on both Maria and Lady Sophia's minds. "What do you mean, Lord Bradstock?"

The gentleman hesitated.

"It is as it sounds, Lady Hayward," he said, spreading his hands. "I will not go into particulars as they are not of any benefit at present. However, what I will say is that these *considerations* are fixed and must be fulfilled entirely. Lord Ridlington will not even consider the fact that he might now have an affection for Lady Maria, for to his mind, such a thing is not required when it comes to matrimony and the like."

Swallowing what was now a rather heavy lump in her throat, Maria looked first at Lady Hayward and then back at Lord Bradstock. The news that Lord Ridlington cared for her was both astonishing and overwhelming but coupled with dismay and despair over both his choices and her own deception. It seemed as though happiness had been only a step away, but now it had been torn from her, leaving a great chasm between herself and Lord Ridlington.

"But I am certain," Lord Bradstock continued, his voice dropping just a little as he put a hand out onto Maria's arm, "that he cares deeply for you, Lady Maria. I have seen how he watches you, seen the smile on his face when he looks into your eyes. When I spoke to him last evening, it was to make it clear to him that I thought his 'requirements' to be nothing short of foolishness. I believe I greatly upset him with what I said, for perhaps it forced him to reconsider what he has always thought to be right. I cannot say. I only hope that he will soon come to his senses and see what is waiting for him."

Tears were threatening and Maria lowered her head, drawing in a shaking breath as Lord Bradstock removed his hand from her arm.

"Thank you for your explanation, Lord Bradstock," she heard Lady Hayward say. "You and I share the same hope, I believe."

Maria dragged in air and forced herself to look back at Lord Bradstock.

"I also thank you," she managed to say, her voice barely louder than a whisper. "I understand now."

Lord Bradstock nodded, smiled and then asked Lady Sophia if she would like to accompany him to the dance floor for the first of their two dances. Lady Sophia nodded and accepted his arm at once, only to give Maria a concerned look, as though she doubted whether or not she ought to go and leave Maria to stand with Lady Hayward.

"Please, do enjoy yourself," Maria said, as Lady Hayward waved her daughter away. "I am quite contented to remain here." Her smile wobbled just a little. "I believe I need a few minutes to regain my composure."

Lady Sophia nodded but held Maria's gaze for a moment longer before she stepped away, leaving Maria to stand with Lady Hayward, feeling as though she were about to wilt to the floor in exhaustion.

"Well, Lady Maria," Lady Hayward said, softly. "It seems as though Lord Ridlington *does*, in fact, have a true affection for you, just as you have for him." Her eyes were gentle as she took Maria's hand for a moment, pressing it encouragingly. "I am certain that, somehow, this can be resolved."

Maria shook her head, having not even a modicum of hope.

"I have deceived him, Lady Hayward and, it seems, he has not been entirely honest with me either. I do not know what these requirements might be, but I am certain that I do not fulfill them. If he is entirely determined not to permit himself to feel a single thing, then what hope do I have?" Her chin lifted as another gentleman she was acquainted with began to make his way towards them, his gaze fixed on her. "Perhaps it would be best if I permitted myself to consider another gentleman entirely."

Lady Hayward's eyes flared wide for a moment, alarm visible in her expression.

"You cannot simply give up, Lady Maria!" she

exclaimed, as Maria forced a smile to her face as Lord Atherton drew near. "If you do so, then –"

"Lord Atherton, good evening."

Maria swept into a curtsey, despising herself as she did so. Lord Atherton was one of the many gentlemen who often came to seek a dance from her and, whilst he was certainly arrogant and, if she were truthful, a rather poor dancer, he was obviously glad of her company.

"Good evening, Lady Maria," he replied, before greeting Lady Hayward who gave something of a stilted reply. "I do hope that your dance card is not yet filled?" His eyes glittered as she handed him her dance card, looking down at it and seeing only Lord Bradstock's name there. "And your waltz is not being kept for another, I hope?"

Recalling that, at a previous ball, she had been required to refuse Lord Atherton the waltz given that she was keeping it for Lord Ridlington, Maria forced a laugh.

"No, indeed, I am not," she replied, as Lord Atherton grinned and then wrote his name there. Quelling the rush of emotions which came with the memory, Maria smiled up at Lord Atherton as he handed her back her card, feigning a delight she did not truly feel.

"Ah," Lord Atherton murmured, looking over her shoulder. "I shall take my leave, given that Lord Brook-mire is advancing upon you!" He chuckled as Maria's smile faded quickly, taking her hand in his in what was a rather overt gesture, before lifting it to his lips. He did not kiss it but instead, simply bowed over it, as Maria caught her breath. "I look forward to our first dance, Lady Maria."

"As do I, Lord Atherton," Maria replied, relieved beyond measure when he let go of her hand. She had not expected him to do such a thing and there came no pleasure from it but rather a deep unsettling unease. "Good evening."

"Good evening."

He stepped away from her and Maria steeled herself for the arrival of Lord Brookmire – only for her to catch sight of Lord Ridlington. He was standing only a few steps away from her, his eyes fixed and his jaw tight as his gaze followed Lord Atherton across the room. And then, he swung that gaze back towards her, his expression never changing as a wall of heat swamped her, sending fire into her cheeks. It was not as though she had done anything wrong in accepting Lord Atherton's offer to dance with her, not as though she had been given any choice when he bent over her hand but, evidently, Lord Ridlington had been watching it all. She did not know what to do, wondering what he was thinking – and what he must think of her.

And then, Lord Ridlington turned smartly on his heel and stepped away, merging into the crowd so that, in only a moment, she could no longer see him. Her heart tore with a new and fresh pain and she found herself starting after him, only for Lady Hayward to put a hand on her arm.

"Allow him to depart," she said softly, clearly aware of Lord Ridlington's presence. "It is good for him to see that you are not without suitors, Lady Maria."

"Lady Maria!"

Lord Brookmire came to stand directly before her,

bowing low before she could even so much as greet him in response.

"I do hope that your dance card is not full?"

Maria blinked rapidly, trying to regain some sort of poise as she unthinkingly slid the card from her wrist and handed it to Lord Brookmire. He practically snatched it from her, muttering something about how he had always attempted to dance with her but so often found her dance card full.

"You must continue through this evening just as usual," Lady Hayward murmured quietly. "Do not allow yourself to become overwhelmed. There is time for that tomorrow."

She smiled sympathetically at Maria, who felt tears begin to burn in the corners of her eyes but blinked them away quickly.

"But Lord Ridlington –"

"Will have a great deal of thinking to do," Lady Hayward interrupted, as Lord Brookmire continued to pore over Maria's dance card, evidently trying to work out which dance would suit him best. "Trust me, Lady Maria. This is for the best."

Maria swallowed her tears and nodded, looking back at Lord Brookmire just as he finished writing his name.

"Wonderful," he said, beaming with great delight as he gave her back her dance card. "The cotillion, Lady Maria! It will begin in a few minutes." He offered her his arm, just as Lord Bradstock and Lady Sophia came back to join them. "Shall we?"

A great burden settled over Maria's heart as she accepted Lord Brookmire's arm, ignoring Lady Sophia's startled look. Walking out, she felt every step grow heavier and slower, and she could not even give a single thought to Lord Brookmire's conversation. She would do as Lady Hayward suggested, even though there was no joy, no happiness, or delight in her heart, praying that, come the morrow, she would be able to think more clearly and, perhaps, know exactly what she was to do next.

CHAPTER TWELVE

Isaac looked at his reflection in the mirror and found that he had changed seemingly overnight. There were deep purple smudges under his eyes, his skin was pale and there seemed to be a great heaviness which was etched into every line of his face. Last evening, he had seen Lady Maria, had seen how she had danced with, smiled at, and seemingly enjoyed the many conversations which the other gentlemen of the *ton* had offered her. One, in particular, had seemed very eager to have her company and had, in fact, lifted Lady Maria's hand to his lips – although whether or not he had kissed it, Isaac did not know. His heart had twisted painfully as he had seen it, realizing that Lady Maria was not without suitors. Indeed, it seemed that she would have no particular difficulty in finding another gentleman to court her, should she wish to.

Does she wish to?

Isaac swallowed hard and turned away from his reflection, his jaw working furiously. He should not care, he told himself. He should not care that Lady Maria might be courted by another, not when it now appeared that she did not meet all of the standards he had set out for her. Of course, he was not certain what it was exactly that she did not satisfy, for he had never asked her as yet, but to know that she had been deceitful in some way or another ought to be enough.

So why then do I feel this heaviness?

"Ridlington, what are you doing?" Isaac turned sharply, seeing Bradstock making his way into the parlor, spreading his hands wide as he did so. "I spoke to Lady Maria last evening and it seems that, although you were present at the same ball as she, you did not see fit to go and speak to her!" Bradstock continued, shaking his head. "What is it that you are doing?"

Grimacing, Isaac gestured to the door.

"I did not ask for company, Bradstock," he grated, his meaning all too clear. "Nor do I require it."

"*That,*" Bradstock stated, without making a single move towards the door, "is entirely untrue. You may think that you do not require my presence here this afternoon, but I assure you that you do." He sat down in a chair and lifted an eyebrow in what was a very pointed gesture. "How else are you to find happiness?"

Isaac shook his head, his brow furrowing as anger burned up his spine.

"I am quite contented," he lied, only for Bradstock to throw back his head and laugh.

"That is blatantly untrue, for I can see the sorrow and the frustration in your eyes, no matter how well you attempt to hide it," he said, tilting his head. "Now, I shall ask you again. What are you doing? Why are you not calling upon Lady Maria?"

Isaac did not know what to say to such a question. He wanted to make some sort of flippant remark in response, wanted to state that Bradstock was quite mistaken, but found that he could not speak another lie. Bradstock sat quietly, his expression unchanged and with a look in his eye which spoke of full awareness of what Isaac was truly feeling.

"There is no reason for you to be absent from her," he said, as Isaac closed his eyes tightly. "I know that you want to speak to her. I know that you want to understand all that she said."

"She spoke of deception," Isaac replied, firmly. "I do not need to know anything else. It is clear that she does not fulfill the requirements I have listed."

"And that is all that matters, is it?" Bradstock replied, with a small shrug. "Your heart, which clearly has a great affection for her, bears no significance?"

Again, Isaac could find nothing to say in response to this. He had never considered that he might come to *feel* something for any lady of his acquaintance and, the truth was, now that he did, now that he was aware of how he felt, he was doing all he could to hide it, to hide from it.

"Go." Bradstock sat forward in his chair, one arm flung out towards the door. "Go and speak to her."

"But..."

"You do not know the reasons for her supposed deception, whatever that specific deceit might have been," Bradstock pointed out.

"I behaved terribly."

Bradstock threw up his hands.

"Apologize!" he exclaimed, as Isaac shook his head. "Explain to her why you behaved in such a way. Tell her the truth, Ridlington." Tilting his head, he looked back at Isaac steadily. "Otherwise happiness which could so easily be yours will be gone from you entirely." Rising from his chair, he came a little nearer to Isaac, looking at him steadily. "What do you feel when you consider a life without Lady Maria?" he asked, as Isaac dropped his gaze, looking away as the question pierced his heart. "What does your spirit cry when you think of her stepping into the arms of another?"

Isaac gritted his teeth, finding the questions deeply unsettling and the thought all the more so.

"You saw how other gentlemen have begun to flock to her," Bradstock continued, his voice now a little quieter. "She will not have to wait long for another prospective suitor."

"Enough!"

Isaac gritted his teeth, one hand swiping the air as he glared at Bradstock. "You have made your point."

"Have I?"

"Yes, you have," Isaac found himself saying, a steady, fierce anger now raging through him but, along with it, came a strange, unsettling determination. "I will go and speak to Lady Maria."

Bradstock's brow lifted.

"Indeed," he said, as though he did not quite believe Isaac. "When?"

Drawing in a long breath, Isaac narrowed his eyes.

"Now," he found himself saying, his chin lifting. "This very moment, if that will please you!"

A small chuckle came from Bradstock, as though Isaac had made a ridiculous statement.

"It will prevent me from irritating you further, if that is what you wish?"

"I do," Isaac retorted, turning his head away from Bradstock. "Now, if you please?"

He spread out one hand towards the door, but Bradstock shook his head.

"I do not think so," he replied, wiggling one finger in Isaac's direction. "I will, of course, take you there in my own carriage, given that it would take time for your own to be prepared. Once I have seen you step inside, then will I be satisfied."

"I am not a child!" Isaac exclaimed, but Bradstock merely shrugged, irritating Isaac all the more. He knew that his friend was entirely steadfast and would not be moved from his chosen course of action. Somewhere between frustration and anger, Isaac stormed towards the door and threw it open before striding out into the hallway. He did not pause to glance at his reflection, nor did he attempt to linger in any way. Instead, he simply barked at one of the footmen that he would return later that afternoon and stepped out into the warm afternoon sun. The fine weather did nothing for his dark mood and, even as he sat down in the carriage, Isaac's spirits did not lift.

"You will need to improve your expression somewhat before you reach Lady Maria," Bradstock said, mildly. "She will think you something of an ogre if you do not."

Isaac said nothing but turned his head so that he might gaze out of the carriage window. His frustration and anger were slowly but surely beginning to melt away and, underneath them, he now found a somewhat unsettling sense of anxiety. He was nervous; terrified, even, of what Lady Maria was going to say – of what *he* had to tell her. Bradstock had somehow known the truth of what Isaac felt, and now expected him to speak the truth to Lady Maria. Could he truly do so, when he was not even entirely certain about all that he felt? He would have to be honest with her about his supposed requirements, would have to express to her the truth about why he had made such standards. The idea of being so very open and even vulnerable with another made Isaac's breathing quicken, and his heart pound in his chest as the carriage came to a stop just outside Lady Hayward's townhouse.

"Lady Sophia is expecting me," Bradstock exclaimed, a broad smile settling across his face as Isaac looked back at him with a frown. "Come now, old boy! You did not truly think that I would simply bring you here for your own sake before driving away again!"

He chuckled and climbed out of the carriage, leaving Isaac to follow suit.

Isaac did not much like the swirling sea which was now his stomach, nor the way that he found his hands clenching and unclenching into tight fists as he climbed the stone steps. This was not what he had wanted to feel. There had always been an expectation that he would be entirely in control of the situation, that he would always know precisely what to do and what to say, being completely certain in his mind that the lady he was to speak to was, in fact, a young lady who met every single one of his requirements.

Now, it seemed, he was not to have what he expected.

"Lord Bradstock and Lord Ridlington," he heard Bradstock say, as they made to step into the house. "I believe we – or at least I – am expected."

The butler murmured something and led them both towards the parlor. Isaac's breathing became labored, his heart pounding furiously as he followed after Bradstock. Part of him wanted to turn around, to state that this idea was no longer wise and that he would not remain, only for him to find himself stepping into the parlor despite those thoughts, to see Lady Maria staring back at him with wide eyes.

"Good afternoon," Bradstock said, cheerfully, as he dropped into a bow. "I know that you were expecting only my company this afternoon, Lady Sophia, but I have found someone who wished very much to join me." He glanced back at Isaac who, forcing his gaze away from Lady Maria, gave a bow although he did not quite manage to say anything. "Lady Hayward, good afternoon."

"Good afternoon," she murmured, as Isaac bowed again towards her, his palms sweaty and spirals of nervousness burrowing their way further into his heart. "We did not expect you, Lord Ridlington."

Isaac looked back at the lady directly and saw the interest in her eyes.

"I apologize for joining you without prior warning," he said, as Lady Hayward's eyes slid towards Lady

Maria. "I – I would very much like to speak to Lady Maria privately, if I may."

Quite certain that everyone could hear just how loudly his heart was beating, Isaac forced himself to look back at Lady Maria, who was now standing stock still, her face a little pale.

"Why do you not go to the music room, Lady Maria?" Lady Hayward suggested, gently. "Take a maid with you. I shall find another maid to remain with Lady Sophia and shall take a few minutes with each of you, to make certain that all is well."

This was said lightly but Isaac did not miss the encouraging glance which was sent in Lady Maria's direction. He could see that Lady Hayward was doing all she could to make certain that her charge did not feel overly anxious about the situation and to make certain that Lady Maria knew that Lady Hayward herself held no concern about the conversation which was now to take place. Taking in a deep breath, Isaac turned his attention back solely to Lady Maria, seeing how she looked back at him steadily, her eyes searching his. There was a hesitation there, a reluctance, perhaps, which spoke of her uncertainty, and Isaac found himself silently willing her to accept his request.

"Very well."

Her words lit a fire in his heart and Lady Hayward smiled, nodded and rose to her feet.

"I will be just a moment," she said, gesturing for Bradstock to seat himself. "Do excuse me. Lady Maria?"

Isaac found himself following Lady Maria and Lady Hayward as they walked from the parlor, with one footman instructed to remain with Bradstock and Lady Sophia, whilst another was dispatched to find not one, but two maids, so that propriety would be maintained. However, Lady Hayward did not remain until the maid arrived, which surprised Isaac greatly. Instead, she simply gestured towards the chairs which littered the room and then stepped back towards the door, stating quietly that she would return within a few minutes.

Isaac nodded and attempted to thank her, but found his tongue now stuck to the roof of his mouth, his lips refusing to move. Lady Hayward's glimmer of a smile and the twinkle in her eye told him that she knew precisely all that he felt and, with a clearing of his throat, he turned back towards Lady Maria, who was now sitting quietly in a chair, her head lowered.

"Lady Maria."

His voice was rasping, his throat aching with a strange tightness that seemed to spread through the rest of his body.

"Lady Maria," he tried again, moving towards her but rather than sitting down opposite, choosing to stand in front of the empty fireplace. "I – I wanted to speak to you."

She looked up at him, her green eyes gentle.

"Oh?"

"There is much that I need to say," he began, as she held his gaze steadily. "First of all, I should never have spoken to you in the manner that I did when you first came to call on me with Lady Hayward." Shame bit down hard and he dropped his head for a moment. "Lord

Bradstock had just taken his leave and what he had said had deeply unsettled me."

Lady Maria pressed her lips together.

"I see."

"But that is not an excuse," Isaac continued, hastily. "I should not have been as cruel nor as improper in what I said to you. I beg that you forgive me, if you can, Lady Maria."

She said nothing but dipped her head for a moment before returning her gaze to his. There was a paleness in her cheeks which Isaac was certain matched his own, a deep uncertainty in her eyes that Isaac could well understand.

"I also apologize for my reluctance in coming to speak to you, Lady Maria," he continued, wondering if she would be willing to talk to him openly about the deception that she had mentioned before. "I know that you were aware of my presence last evening, just as I was aware of yours. I –" Running one hand over his forehead, he blew out an exasperated breath. "I should have come to speak to you, Lady Maria, but in my own foolishness, I did not."

"But I can understand your reasons for wishing to remain apart from me, Lord Ridlington," came the swift reply. "I cannot imagine what you must think, knowing that I spoke of deception." Her pallor was now a little grey, her eyes closing tightly for a long moment. "But I shall not step back from the truth now, not if you wish to hear it?"

When she opened her eyes, Isaac saw the depths of fear there and found himself feeling almost sorry for her, as though part of him did not want her to have to tell him the truth for fear of what she would have to endure because of it.

"I should like to know," he answered, honestly, making his way to a chair opposite and sitting down, entirely unaware of the small maid who had crept into the room and sat down in the corner. "I shall not judge you harshly, Lady Maria, I assure you."

Her halfhearted smile was not one of confidence.

"I fear that you shall, Lord Ridlington," she replied softly, "but I will not blame you for anything that you choose to do thereafter." Taking in a deep breath, she looked back at him steadily, her gaze clear, and her expression one of calm determination. "I am not the young lady you believe me to be."

A tight hand grasped hard at Isaac's heart but, with an effort, he stemmed the many questions which began to pour from it, choosing instead just to listen to what she had to say.

"You believe that I play the pianoforte well, that my drawings contain a good deal of promise." The words which came from Lady Maria now held a touch of bitterness, making Isaac frown hard. "You believe that I have no interest in anything other than fashion plates, in gossip, and in what gowns I am to wear. You think that I read novels, that I fill my head with nonsense, and that, in every way, I am a vapid, unassuming young lady of the *ton*." Her eyes became a little hard as she looked back at him, her chin lifting a notch. "But the truth is, Lord Ridlington, I have placed upon myself an appearance of such things."

Isaac swallowed hard, his jaw tight.

"Why would you do such a thing?"

She threw up her hands as a furious anger poured into her expression.

"Because, Lord Ridlington, I have failed entirely."

"Failed?" he repeated, a little taken aback. "In what regard?"

It took Lady Maria a moment or two to answer, such was the sadness which had etched itself into her expression. When she turned her head to look back at him, Isaac was overcome by the sorrow in her eyes, finding himself half out of his chair as though he were desperate to comfort her, before forcing himself to sit back.

"My sisters have each made an excellent match, very soon after their arrival in London, Lord Ridlington," she said, a slight coldness to her tone as though she wanted to disassociate herself from any pain which came with such a statement. "They have done very well indeed. However, I have been in London for a spring Season and have spent the autumn and winter months here also, before returning this Season. And yet, I did not have even a single offer of courtship during those previous visits." Her lips flattened for a long moment, and her hands were clasped tightly together as she held them in her lap. "A remark was made during the very first ball which I attended this Season, which made me realize that the reason for my lack of success was entirely my own fault."

"I cannot imagine that —"

"I am a bluestocking, Lord Ridlington," she interrupted before he could say more. "I have, prior to this Season, thought nothing of expressing my opinions, of giving my thoughts, and of being eager to further my knowledge of certain subjects." She shook her head and looked away, color beginning to rise in her cheeks. "It seems, however, that such behavior is not welcomed by the *beau monde*. Therefore, I chose, this Season, to put on a pretense, to hide the fact that I am well-read and have a great eagerness to further my knowledge all the more. Instead of speaking of the Corn Laws or expressing my opinion on the Luddite uprising, I remained entirely silent and pretended that I knew nothing of them." She lifted one shoulder in a half shrug as Isaac sat stock still, a coldness pouring over him as he listened. "And I have been entirely successful," she finished, loosening the tight grasp of her hands and then spreading them wide. "Gentlemen of the *ton* have considered me to be just what they expect a young lady of the *ton* to be. I have had more dances, more conversation, and more interest than ever before. To have gentlemen calling upon me, to have them show a particular interest, has been a very great relief, removing from me the fear that I shall become a spinster aunt who requires the aid of her sisters in order to live a vaguely satisfying life." Her chin wobbled suddenly as she looked back at him, her shoulders slumping just a little. "But then, Lord Ridlington, I discovered myself to be more than a little caught up with you."

The shock of her words had not left Isaac as yet. It poured through him like a heavy burst of rain, soaking him to the skin. Lady Maria was *entirely* unsuitable, it seemed. She was the very essence of everything he did *not* require and yet, there came with that acknowledgment a clear and considered understanding of all that she had done.

"Those drawings?" he found himself saying, looking up at her. Lady Maria closed her eyes and let out a shuddering breath.

"Lady Sophia encouraged me to take her own in place of my dire attempt," she stated, without hiding the truth. "When she and I played together on the pianoforte, it was Lady Sophia's performance which you heard, rather than my own." She shook her head, looking down. "I realized that I had to tell you the truth, Lord Ridlington, given all that I now felt for you."

Those words slammed hard into Isaac, forcing him to catch his breath. He could not pretend that he did not feel an attachment to Lady Maria and yet, the shock of what she had told him was still overwhelming him.

"I thought that you were quite perfect, Lady Maria," he found himself saying. "I – I came to London having detailed a list of the exact requirements needed for any young lady whom I might consider as my wife, and I thought that you fulfilled them all." Surprise filled Lady Maria's eyes, but Isaac dropped his gaze, a smattering of guilt now running through him. "But now it seems that you do not," he found himself saying, his words heavy and filled with a gravitas which seemed to spread out across the room. His eyes lifted back to hers, a heavy weight in his soul. "A bluestocking?"

She nodded, not stepping back from that particular definition.

"I am aware that to be such carries a good deal of mockery with it, Lord Ridlington," she said, her expression and her voice a little clearer now, "but I have no shame in being so. I have read a great deal, learned a great deal, and I have every intention of continuing in such a manner." Her color rose all the more but she did not look away from him. "I did not give any real thought to what I might do should a gentleman seek to court me, did not really understand what it might feel like to pretend to be someone I was not, but in the end, it has placed me in such a great tangle of emotions that I deeply regret all that I have done. Although," she finished, softly, "that does not mean that anything I have come to *feel*, Lord Ridlington, is not entirely genuine."

Isaac knew precisely what she was saying but found himself shaking his head, before running two hands through his hair. A small groan escaped his lips as he leaned forward, his elbows on his knees and his eyes staring, unseeingly, at the floor.

"I am aware that this must come as a great shock," he heard Lady Maria say. "If I could remove the pain and confusion from you, then I would do so in an instant." There came a short pause and Isaac closed his eyes tightly, feeling his emotions tug and pull at him, each one determined to take the strongest hold. "When Lady Hayward told me of your note, of your request to court me, I knew then that I could not go on. I had to be truthful with you, given that my heart was already engaged, Lord Ridlington. It remains so, even though I know very well that what I have done might well push you away from me entirely."

"You do not fulfill my requirements." His head lifted, his voice rasping as he looked back into her face. "I have a list," he found himself saying, as he rose to his feet, beginning to tick them off on his fingers. "Any lady I consider must be of particular standing, with a fine dowry and inheritance." He continued to speak of each and every requirement he had made for a woman to even be considered, seeing how Lady Maria's eyes widened all the more, her color beginning to fade away as he finally came to an end. "And I thought that you, Lady Maria, satisfied them all. I came to you in the hope of courtship and, thereafter, a betrothal. But now it seems that I have been quite mistaken in what I have thought of you."

Lady Maria took in a long breath, closing her eyes tightly. When she opened them again, Isaac fully expected to see tears glistening there but, much to his astonishment, he saw nothing other than a clear, calm steadiness.

"Why have you made such a set of standards, Lord Ridlington?" she asked, softly, but Isaac shook his head, turning away from her for a moment as he rose to begin pacing up and down the floor.

"Before he died, my father told me to do so," he stated, firmly, remembering the words which had been spoken to him so long ago. "He wed a lady he believed he cared for, only to find that his years with her were filled with nothing but strife." He turned his head to look back at Lady Maria, seeing how she sat in her chair, her hands now clasped lightly in her lap, her eyes watching him carefully. "I do not want to endure the same."

"Do you believe, then, that what I say I feel for you within my heart is entirely false, Lord Ridlington?" He could not answer her, turning back to face her only to see that she had risen to her feet and was now stepping closer to him. "Do you expect that what I feel will simply fade away?" she asked, as Isaac found himself fixed to the floor, quite unable to move. "That this affection, this eager desire to be close to you, will simply come to naught?" She tilted her head and looked up at him, her beauty more evident to him than ever before. "What I feel for you, Lord Ridlington, has been what has forced me to speak so. I could not have continued to deceive you, even though it would have been very simple indeed to do so." A small, sad smile pulled at one corner of her mouth. "Instead, I chose to tell you the truth so that you would know me as I truly am, knowing that the consequences which such a truth might bring would be great and difficult to bear."

"I – I can see what you are trying to express," Isaac said, his throat constricting as she took a small step closer, finding his skin prickling all over with the awareness of just how near to him she was now. "But I cannot be certain, Lady Maria."

"But does certainty have to bear such a tight hold upon you, Lord Ridlington?" she asked, her expression gentle, her eyes searching his own until he felt as though his very soul were being slowly uncovered. "When it comes to matters of the heart, there must be a trust between two people. A trust that what they feel will continue to grow rather than fade away and that, during times of difficulty, their affection – their love – will be the only thing they cling to."

Isaac closed his eyes, no longer able to look at her.

"You believe that I feel an affection for you, Lady Maria?" he asked, just as a gentle laugh escaped from her.

"I do," she said, softly, as he let out a long, slow breath. "And I believe that you are greatly confused by it, Lord Ridlington."

Hearing footsteps in the hallway, Isaac opened his eyes again, only to see Lady Maria sitting back in her chair, her hands clasped gently. Clearing his throat, he inclined his head and made to take his leave, only for Lady Maria to hold up one hand, silencing him for a moment.

"I will tell you now, Lord Ridlington, that there is a love within my heart which is solely for you," she said, speaking with more openness than ever before. "I love you." Her smile was gentle, spreading warmth and happiness through her expression. "I find your list of requirements, whilst understandable, to be entirely bereft of any sort of emotion and thus, whilst I know that I fail to fulfill them entirely, I can only pray that you will set them aside and will, instead, consider what is within your own heart instead. Trust yourself, Lord Ridlington. Trust *me*, if you are able. I swear that I shall never turn from you." A small smile pulled at her mouth, her eyes softening all the more. "Although I fear that you will have to accept that I shall never be anything other than a bluestocking."

Isaac could not find any words to reply to Lady Maria's remark, feeling his heart yearning for her and yet struggling to know what to say or what to do. Part of him wanted to fall at her feet and to proclaim that he had been nothing other than foolish, whilst the other part told

him to retreat; to return home, and to allow the shock of
what she had told him finally dissipate.

"Lord Ridlington?"

He turned to see Lady Hayward standing framed in
the doorway.

"I – I was just taking my leave of Lady Maria," he
said, turning from the lady as Lady Hayward stepped out
of his path. "Good afternoon to you, Lady Hayward."

"Good afternoon."

Her voice was soft, drifting after him as he walked
quickly down the hallway and back towards the front
door.

I shall never be anything other than a bluestocking.

Lady Maria's final words caught at his heart as he
stepped back outside into the sunshine. They wrapped
themselves around him, tying themselves to him without
any obvious intention of letting him go. Isaac closed his
eyes tightly for a moment, pinching the bridge of his nose
before, finally, he turned on his heel and marched
hurriedly down the street.

CHAPTER THIRTEEN

Lady Hayward smiled warmly as Maria entered the room, dressed and prepared for the evening's assembly.

"You look very well indeed, Lady Maria," Lady Hayward told her, as Maria smiled back at her. "Although I must ask how you *truly* are?"

Maria gave her chaperone a small smile.

"I will not pretend that my heart is not aching terribly, nor that my mind is not whirling with a great many thoughts," she replied, as Lady Hayward nodded in understanding. "But I shall say that I am contented enough to have left the decision entirely in Lord Ridlington's hands. I have told him everything and now there is nothing left for me to either say or do."

Lady Hayward nodded in understanding.

"You told him all that he needed to know," she said, softly. "I am only sorry that he did not give you the answer you hoped."

"He may yet," Maria replied, allowing the small sense

of hope which had filled her as she had spoken to Lord Ridlington to grow just a little more. "I will say that the shock in his expression at realizing that I was a blue-stocking rather that the perfect young lady of the *ton* that he expected was rather severe." Her lips twisted. "Although, should he ask me what I thought of his specific 'requirements' for any such young lady, I would tell him that I thought them all entirely ridiculous."

Lady Hayward chuckled.

"I am glad to hear it," she said, with a shake of her head.

Last evening, Maria had told her in detail all that Lord Ridlington had said, including the fact that his requirements were to be fulfilled in their entirety. Lady Hayward had expressed her surprise that Maria was not angry that she had been judged so, but Maria had not felt any such thing. In fact, she had been so relieved to express the truth from her own heart to Lord Ridlington that nothing he had said had caused her any upset. Yes, she thought his standards and his list of specifications for his potential bride were ridiculous and would bring him more difficulty than good, but, as they had been speaking, she had seen the confusion in his eyes and had known that he was questioning his own heart and his own thinking. That had been what had given her the sense of hope that perhaps after some time to consider, he might realize that there was a great happiness to be had if only he could set aside his own precon-ceptions.

"Has he written to you?" Maria turned to see Lady Sophia hurrying into the room, her eyes filled with excitement, her hands flapping just a little. "Has he sent a note?"

Maria shook her head.

"No, he has not," she replied, as the hope faded from Lady Sophia's eyes. "But I did not expect him to," she added. "It was only yesterday afternoon that all was said between us. There is much for him to consider, I am sure."

"You are so very calm," Lady Sophia replied, with a shake of her head. "I do not think I would be so."

Tilting her head just a little, Maria smiled back at her friend, her heart lifting with happiness for her.

"Lord Bradstock is to be present this evening, I understand?"

A flush crept into Lady Sophia's cheeks.

"He is," she said, quietly. "I have not told you as yet, but Lord Bradstock has asked Mama's permission to court me." Her eyes glowed with happiness as Maria reached to grasp her friend's hand, truly delighted for her. "Of course, Mama has agreed." Her smile faded for a moment as she looked into Maria's eyes. "I do hope my news does not trouble you."

"Trouble me?" Maria repeated, now throwing her arms around Lady Sophia in a warm embrace. "I am not at all troubled! Indeed, I am more than a little delighted!" Stepping back, she saw the relief pour into Lady Sophia's expression. "I am sure that he will make you very happy."

"I believe you are correct, Lady Maria," Lady Hayward murmured, coming to join them both. "Now, perhaps this evening, we might find the very same happiness for yourself also?"

One eyebrow lifted but Maria shook her head.

"I do not even know if he is to be in attendance and, if he is, what he will say," she answered, as Lady Hayward looked back at her steadily. "But I am quite prepared to enjoy myself regardless. I will wait for his response and, whatever it may be, I shall accept it."

Lady Hayward pressed Maria's hand without a word before turning to make her way towards the door. Maria followed her, her heart holding that same, flickering hope which had entered it yesterday afternoon when Lord Ridlington had come to speak to her. Just what would this evening bring?

"You are very kind, Lord Atherton."

Maria bobbed a quick curtsey as the gentleman handed her back her dance card, a broad smile settling on his face. He appeared almost proud to have been the one to steal the waltz from any other gentleman who might have been eager to obtain it, but Maria did not think particularly highly of him. He was, to her mind, much too arrogant and self-interested, even though in every other aspect, he appeared to be quite the gentleman. He was not a rogue, certainly, and she was sure that there would be many young ladies who now struggled to contain their envy that he had picked Maria's waltz.

"I look forward to it, Lady Maria," Lord Atherton replied, bowing low. "Do excuse me."

"But of course."

Her gaze drifted about the room aimlessly, even

184 | ROSE PEARSON

though, within her heart, Maria knew that she was trying to find any sign of Lord Ridlington's presence. Either he was not present this evening, or he *was* in attendance and, as yet, had chosen not to come to speak to her. The hope that she had carried now began to fade, although it flickered on in determination, doing all it could to stay alight.

"Are you quite well, Lady Maria?"

Maria looked back at Lady Sophia, who was looking at her with a wide-eyed, searching gaze.

"I have not seen him this evening," Maria replied, a little heavily. "I had thought that..."

She looked down at her dance card and saw the many names written there, realizing that, very soon indeed, she would have to step out with the first gentleman for the first dance of the evening. Almost all of her dances were taken and, with Lord Atherton taking the waltz, Maria knew that there was no hope of dancing it solely with Lord Ridlington.

"He may yet appear," Lady Sophia replied softly, as Maria nodded, attempting to find a little more courage and not to give in to despair. "He may yet –"

"Or he may think me quite ridiculous and will not so much as come near to me," Maria replied, a trifle stiffly. "And if such a thing was to occur, then I must accept it without hesitation. After all, it is precisely what I deserve, given what I chose to do." Seeing Lady Sophia about to protest, Maria held up one hand, silencing her before she could begin. "Truly, you need not," she said, softly. "I am very able to admit that some of what I chose to do was very selfish indeed." One shoulder lifted and then fell again, as Maria saw the sympathy in Lady Sophia's face. "As I have said, whatever Lord Ridlington decides, I shall accept it, no matter how difficult it might be."

"I do hope that you will not have to wait too long," Lady Sophia replied, kindly. "I..."

Her eyes widened as she looked over Maria's shoulder at something – or someone – behind her.

Maria's heart began to quicken as she took in Lady Sophia's expression. She did not need to ask who it was that was approaching, already fully aware that Lord Ridlington, the very gentleman they had been speaking of, was drawing near.

"Good evening, Lady Hayward, Lady Sophia, Lady Maria."

Turning quickly, Maria placed a smile on her lips and looked directly up at Lord Ridlington, seeing the cloudy grey of his eyes as he gazed back at her.

"Good evening," she replied, aware of just how tremulous her voice was. "I – I am glad to see you, Lord Ridlington."

He did not reply to this remark but, rather, simply smiled at her, before turning back to Lady Sophia.

"Your dance card, Lady Sophia?" he asked, before looking to Maria again. "And yours also, Lady Maria?"

Maria wanted to grasp his arm, to give him a slight shake and to demand to know what it was he had decided about her, to tell him that she did not think she could wait even another moment before he did so, but she knew that to do so would be more than improper. He had come to speak to her, at least, and was now asking to dance with her, so surely that could not mean that he intended to step away from her for good?

Although it may just be that your acquaintance will continue but not develop into anything more, she told herself, handing him her dance card. It was also not an appropriate time for him to speak to her at length, she realized, although if he had wished to, then surely, he might have begged Lady Hayward to accompany them for a short turn about the room? The assembly was very busy indeed and certainly, no-one would overhear them should they speak at length.

Sighing inwardly, Maria watched Lord Ridlington as he bowed his head over her dance card, seeing the flickering frown and wondering what it might mean. Was he frustrated that she had not very many dances left for him to choose from?

"Wonderful." Lord Ridlington handed her back her dance card and then did the same for Lady Sophia. "I look forward to dancing with both of you this evening." He inclined his head. "Until then."

Maria stared after him, astonishment filling her as she watched Lord Ridlington move away from them all. Even Lady Hayward appeared quite overcome for her mouth was a little ajar whilst Lady Sophia's brows knotted together in an angry frown.

"Well!" she exclaimed, drawing Maria's attention. "Whatever was that for?"

"It appears Lord Ridlington wishes to dance," Maria replied, looking down at her dance card and seeing that he had taken only the cotillion, which came before the waltz, leaving one other dance entirely free. "Only the one dance with me this evening, however." Her heart sank low in her chest and she felt tears begin to push into her eyes. "I think this makes things quite clear."

Lady Hayward tutted loudly, her eyes a little narrowed as she continued to watch Lord Ridlington disappear into the crowd.

"That is not at all clear," she said, as Maria sniffed as quietly as she could, attempting to force her tears back. "No, he will *have* to speak to you, Lady Maria. He cannot simply write his name down for one dance and expect you to ascertain his intentions!" She looked back at Maria, her anger fading as she realized just how upset Maria now was. "Come, my dear, have a little more courage. It may be that he has not yet decided –"

"You are very kind to try to encourage me, but I believe that I know what he intends now," Maria interrupted, her hope now dying slowly as Lady Hayward put a gentle hand on her arm, in an obvious attempt to comfort her. "He does not wish to pain me with deep explanations and thus hopes that such a gesture will make things quite plain."

"Lady Maria, the first dance is to be ours!"

Maria pasted a smile to her lips that she did not feel and greeted Lord Bannister with forced enthusiasm.

"But of course, Lord Bannister," she replied, as Lady Hayward watched her closely, her hand dropping from Maria's arm. "I had not forgotten!"

Lord Bannister chuckled and offered Maria his arm, which she took quickly, keeping her smile fixed in place as they walked together out onto the floor. But inwardly, her heart was crying out with pain, tears held back by nothing other than sheer force of will as a deep sense of loss ripped through her.

≈

"THE COTILLION, LADY MARIA."

Maria had known that this moment was coming but it was even more painful than she had expected. To look into Lord Ridlington's face and to see the smile on his lips and yet the cold determination in his eyes brought her nothing other than sorrow and regret. She knew now that he had chosen to set her aside. Her deception had been too great and, for whatever reason, his requirements were of greater importance than what was within his heart. She had to accept that, just as she had told herself she would, but now to step out with him, to dance with him as though they were only quite happily acquainted, was almost too difficult for her to bear.

"But of course, Lord Ridlington."

Maria dared not look at Lady Hayward nor Lady Sophia as she stepped out with Lord Ridlington, knowing that there would be such compassion in their expressions that her tears might begin to flow. She had to keep her composure for the rest of the evening until she could finally permit her tears to release in the comfort of her own company.

"You look very well this evening, Lady Maria."

Stepping back into her place, Maria said nothing in response but merely gave him a small smile, averting her gaze after only a moment. All that could have been, seemed now to be torn from her grasp, and yet Maria knew that the consequences of her deceit were entirely her own doing.

It was with great relief that she heard the music begin. Nothing was said between them for the entirety of the dance and Maria chose to focus solely on her steps, making certain not to make a single mistake as she danced with Lord Ridlington. Very rarely did she catch his eye and, the times that she did so, she saw no happiness in his expression. Rather, he appeared to be watching her with something of a darkness about his expression, his eyes like thunderclouds, and his jaw held tight. Maria did not want to ask him what it was he thought of, fearing that the answer would be related to just how poorly she had treated him.

And then the dance came to an end, and Maria found herself greatly relieved that she would not have to stand up with him again. This was an end to their acquaintance now, she supposed. They might greet each other and, on occasion, dance together, but there was no need for anything more. Dropping into a curtsey, she took Lord Ridlington's proffered arm and began to walk alongside him.

"You will forgive me, Lady Maria."

Maria looked up in surprise, seeing how Lord Ridlington's jaw had tightened all the more.

"Forgive you?" she repeated, warily. "What do you mean?"

He looked back at her, drawing her into the crowd as Maria caught her breath, realizing that they were nowhere near Lady Hayward.

"I will not return you to Lady Hayward, not when I

know that you are promised to *Atherton*." That word was practically spat from his lips, startling her with his vehemence. "I should have sought you out sooner. I should have made certain to be at your side the moment that you came into the ballroom. Perhaps then I would have been able to take the waltz."

Maria's heart was beating so furiously that she found herself struggling to breathe, but it was not with fright or terror. Rather, she found herself almost excited about what he was intending, realizing slowly that everything she had thought was not as it had appeared.

"I wanted to waltz with you, Lady Maria," he said, turning towards her. "If I keep you with me, then Atherton cannot do so." A small smile tugged at his lips, pulling the darkness from his eyes and making Maria realize that the thunderclouds she had seen in his expression came from his dislike of Lord Atherton, not from any displeasure with her. "You will step out with me, will you not?"

"I will," Maria breathed, one hand flattened against her heart. "But Lord Ridlington, what does this mean? Why have you sought me out in such a fashion?" She turned to face him, heedless of those around them. "What of your requirements?"

Lord Ridlington shook his head, grimacing.

"Lady Maria, I have found myself torn in two directions," he said, speaking with a new sense of vulnerability that Maria could not help but be drawn to. "I have heard the words of my father echo in my heart as the memories of the strain and the tension which flooded my father's household continued to hold fast over me. The list of requirements I created was an attempt to make certain that such a thing would not occur with me. I wanted a wife who was, in all things, just as I expected and would not display any..." He bit his lip. "Any ill manners or the like, which might cause difficulty. I did not expect affection nor even to care particularly for her, but presumed that our marriage would be a quiet yet settled one, where the heir would be produced and all would be well." His hand reached out and settled on hers, in full view of all those around them. "And then, I met you."

"But I was playing a part," Maria replied, softly. "You know very well that I was not all that you believed me to be."

"And somehow," he answered swiftly, "that brings me no concern. You were right when you stated that, if we were to continue in the full knowledge of each other's character, then I should have to trust that what you have stated you feel for me is not only true but will continue."

Maria swallowed hard, her eyes fixed on him as her breath caught in her chest.

"Do you believe that you can do so, Lord Ridlington?"

Opening his mouth to answer, Lord Ridlington hesitated, turning his head back towards the dance floor as the waltz was announced. Maria's hand tightened in his, feeling as though she were standing on the very edge of a precipice without knowing which way she would fall. The music began and still, Lord Ridlington stood without speaking, his eyes now turning back towards her as he held her gaze, his lips pressing together hard for a moment.

"Come, Lady Maria."

His voice was soft and filled with a tenderness which made Maria's heart leap with both hope and anticipation. She did not even think about Lady Hayward, nor about Lady Sophia, who was, at present, no doubt wondering where she had gone. Instead, she simply walked with Lord Ridlington as he led her out to the dance floor, his hand clasping her waist as they began to dance. The music seemed to swirl around them, lifting Maria into a state of such great exaltation that she could not keep from smiling, seeing how Lord Ridlington smiled back at her.

"I think, Lord Ridlington, this must mean that you have forgiven me for my deception?" she asked, her heart pounding furiously. "I know that it was very wrong of me to deceive you, but I must pray that you can understand."

"I am only sorry that you felt required to do so," came the reply. "Although, I will confess that, perhaps, I should be grateful for it, as, should you not have perpetrated your deception, I would not have found myself eager to draw close to you, given that I would have thought you entirely unsuitable."

She laughed, her fear and her upset gone from her entirely.

"And now, Lord Ridlington?"

The tenderness in his eyes spoke to her heart, the waltz continuing as they danced together.

"Now, Lady Maria, I find myself quite lost," he said, surprising her with his choice of words. "I have chosen to give in to what I feel, to consider that my affection for you is so great that it will overcome any fear that lingers."

A small flicker of doubt lodged itself into Maria's heart.

"Fear?"

"Fear that I am making a mistake," he told her, honestly. "Fear that I am turning from the right path. But," he continued, as Maria's smile faded just a little, "the more that I look into your eyes, the more that I realize the truth of your affection, the more that fear is pushed aside."

Maria's expression cleared and the music finally began to come to a close.

"Then, Lord Ridlington, given that you have chosen to set aside your requirements and that I have set aside my deception, what is there for us now?"

Lord Ridlington did not release her, even though other couples were now bowing and curtseying to each other, but instead simply held her hand in his, looking deeply into her eyes.

And then, he lifted her hand to his lips and kissed it gently, sending a flurry of heat all through Maria.

"If I had the courage, I would do more this," he murmured, as Maria's breath caught in her chest. "But I would not like to bring down the wrath of your father upon my head before I have even the chance to meet him!"

Maria laughed softly and dropped into a curtsey, not wanting to draw too much unwanted attention from the other members of the *ton*.

"I assure you, he will not refuse anything you might ask of him, Lord Ridlington," she replied, feeling almost giddy with happiness. "Rather, he will be nothing other than relieved."

"Then I will write to him this very evening," came the reply, as he turned her back in the direction of Lady Hayward who was, Maria noted, watching them with very sharp eyes indeed, although Maria was certain that there was a ghost of a smile playing about her mouth. "Come now, let me return you to Lady Hayward before she marches over here and pulls you from the dance floor!"

Maria laughed and, placing her hand on his arm, walked back towards her chaperone, feeling such delight that she was certain everyone could see just how joyful her heart was. Everything, it seemed, was finally coming together to bring both herself and Lord Ridlington to a place of contented happiness, and Maria was now quite certain that nothing could bring their joy to an end.

EPILOGUE

"**Y**ou have a letter, my Lord."

Isaac rose from his chair at once and grasped the sealed letter from his butler, before dismissing him quickly.

"Good gracious!" Bradstock exclaimed, as he broke open the seal. "Have you some sort of great urgency driving you?"

"I do."

Isaac did not say more but, unfolding the letter, read the few lines quickly, only to sink down into a chair and, letting out a long breath, throw one hand through his hair. He had written to the Duke of Landon some days ago and, until now, had not received a reply. Despite Lady Maria's assurances, he had found himself struggling with worry, fearful that the Duke would, for whatever reason, refuse to accept him as an appropriate suitor for his daughter.

"Ah, so this must be the long-awaited reply from the Duke of Landon," Bradstock murmured, as Isaac lifted his gaze to his friend. "I do hope that you have been successful in your entreaty."

Relief spread through him and a broad smile settled upon Isaac's face as Bradstock began to laugh, picking up his brandy and toasting Isaac's success before throwing it back in a single gulp.

"Thank you," Isaac replied, feeling his heart pounding with such a furious joy that it seemed to rob him of strength, leaving him feeling a little weak as he sat back in his chair and let out a long, slow breath. "I – I must go to Lady Maria at once. At this very moment!"

Bradstock grinned and rose from his chair.

"Then shall we take my carriage?" he asked, as Isaac folded the letter again and pushed it into his pocket. "Given that my betrothed will, no doubt, be very glad to see me, I would be very glad to accompany you there."

Isaac chuckled and rose to his feet.

"I am sure that Lady Sophia would be *delighted* to see you," he replied, as they made their way to the door. "Thank you, Bradstock."

"Lady Maria."

Isaac rose from his chair, all too aware that there was no-one else present. Lady Hayward had made some sort of excuse which Isaac had paid very little attention to, and both Lady Sophia and Bradstock had insisted upon accompanying her. It was all too apparent that they wanted to give Isaac and Lady Maria a few minutes to discuss Isaac's news and, for that, Isaac had to admit that he was very grateful indeed.

"I have received a reply from your father."

Lady Maria was on her feet at once, her hands grasping the letter as he held it out to her. Isaac watched her closely as she unfolded it, seeing the way her smile began to spread across her face as she read the few lines the Duke had written in reply. When she looked up at him, her eyes were shining with happiness – a happiness which also now filled Isaac's heart entirely.

"Then he has agreed," she said softly, before setting the letter down on the table next to them. "There is nothing further you need do, Lord Ridlington."

"Save for this," he answered, reaching out one hand and grasping her own in his. The way her eyes flared made him smile, the color in her cheeks matching the fire which she had lit within his own heart. At that moment, Isaac realized just how foolish he had been with his ridiculous requirements. Whilst a lady might have fulfilled every single one of them, she might never have made him feel as he did at this moment. "Lady Maria, I should very much like to court you," he said, speaking with as much affection as he could express. "But not only that, my dear lady. After an appropriate time, I have every expectation of seeking your hand in marriage, for I do not think that I shall ever again find such a wonderful creature as you. You have shown me the truth of my fears, have knocked my specifications to the ground, and, in doing so, have opened my heart to something which I have never before even considered." His other hand pressed lightly against his heart. "You have opened it up to love, Lady Maria," he continued, softly. "I know now that I love you most ardently. The thought of never being by your side again is one that I cannot even bear to consider. Should we court, then it will be with the prospect of matrimony in our future, for there is nothing I want more than to make you my bride."

Lady Maria reached up and touched his cheek, her gentle fingers searing his skin.

"Even though I am a bluestocking?" she asked, quietly teasing him. "Even though I do not play the pianoforte well and simply cannot even attempt to paint with any degree of expertise?"

"Even though that may be true," he replied, laughing, "I will still ask you to accept me, Lady Maria." He took a step closer and Lady Maria dropped her hand to his shoulder, her eyes almost dazzling him. "I love you."

"And I promise to love you with my whole heart," came the reply, as her other hand settled around his neck as she pulled herself a little closer to him. "And I am certain that we shall have many a discussion on the Corn Laws, or the history of the Luddite uprising!"

She laughed as Isaac pulled her tight against him, his hands now about her waist.

"I shall be grateful for every moment of it," he told her, truthfully. "For you have shown me just how foolish I have been and what I would lose should I reject all that I felt."

"But you did not," she said, softly, her fingers twining into his hair and sending flurries of heat all through him. "You have opened your heart to me, have forgiven my deception, and now see what happiness is before us!"

"Happiness that will forever be ours," he promised before he bent his head to kiss her.

I HOPE you enjoyed Lady Maria's story. Had I lived during Regency times, I might have been like her in that I can't draw, play piano, or sing and thus, would not have fared well in the marriage mart! I am glad she found someone to love despite her bluestocking tendencies.

If you haven't read it yet, please check out some marriage of convenience stories in The Spinsters Guild series. Here is the first in the series A New Beginning. Read one for the first couple chapters!

A SNEAK PEEK OF A NEW BEGINNING

CHAPTER ONE

"Good evening, Miss Taylor."

Miss Emily Taylor, daughter to the Viscount Chesterton, kept her gaze low to the ground, her stomach knotting. The gentleman who had greeted her was, at this present moment, looking at her with something akin to a leer, his balding head already gleaming in the candlelight.

"Good evening, Lord Smithton," she murmured, hearing the grunt from her father than indicated she should be doing more than simply acknowledging the gentleman's presence. The last thing Emily wished to do, however, was to encourage the man any further. He was, to her eyes, grotesque, and certainly not a suitable match for someone who had only recently made her debut, even *if* he was a Marquess.

"Emily is delighted to see you this evening," her father said, giving Emily a small push forward. "I am certain she will be glad to dance with you whenever you wish!"

Emily closed her eyes, resisting the urge to step back

from the fellow, in the knowledge that should she do so, her father would make certain that consequences would follow. She could not bring herself to speak, almost feeling Lord Smithton's eyes roving over her form as she opened her eyes and kept her gaze low.

"You know very well that I would be more than pleased to accompany you to the floor," Lord Smithton said, his voice low and filled with apparent longing. Emily suppressed a shudder, forcing herself to put her hand out and let her dance card drop from her wrist. Lord Smithton, however, did not grasp her dance card but took her hand in his, making a gasp escape from her mouth. The swift intake of breath from behind her informed Emily that she was not alone in her surprise and shock, for her mother also was clearly very upset that Lord Smithton had behaved in such an improper fashion. Her father, however, said nothing and, in the silence that followed, allowed himself a small chuckle.

Emily wanted to weep. It was obvious that her father was not about to say a single word about Lord Smithton's improper behavior. Instead, it seemed he was encouraging it. Her heart ached with the sorrow that came from having a father who cared so little for her that he would allow impropriety in front of so many of the *beau monde*. Her reputation could be stained from such a thing, whispers spread about her, and yet her father would stand by and allow them to go about her without even a twinge of concern.

Most likely, this was because his intention was for Emily to wed Lord Smithton. It had been something Emily had begun to suspect during these last two weeks, for Lord Smithton had been present at the same social gatherings as she had attended with her parents, and her father had always insisted that she greet him. Nothing had been said as yet, however, which came as something of a relief, but deep down, Emily feared that her father would simply announce one day that she was engaged to the old, leering Lord Smithton.

"Wonderful," Lord Smithton murmured, finally letting go of Emily's hand and grasping her dance card. "I see that you have no others as yet, Miss Taylor."

"We have only just arrived," said Emily's mother, from just behind Emily. "That is why –"

"I am certain that Lord Smithton does not need to know such things," Lord Chesterton interrupted, silencing Emily's mother immediately. "He is clearly grateful that Emily has not yet had her head turned by any other gentleman as yet."

Closing her eyes tightly, Emily forced herself to breathe normally, aware of how Lord Smithton chuckled at this. She did not have any feelings of attraction or even fondness for Lord Smithton but yet her father was stating outright that she was interested in Lord Smithton's attentions!

"I have chosen the quadrille, the waltz and the supper dance, Miss Taylor."

Emily's eyes shot open, and she practically jerked back the dance card from Lord Smithton's hands, preventing him from finishing writing his name in the final space. Her father stiffened beside her, her mother gasping in shock, but Emily did not allow either reaction to prevent her from keeping her dance card away from Lord Smithton.

"I am afraid I cannot permit such a thing, Lord Smithton," she told him plainly, her voice shaking as she struggled to find the confidence to speak with the strength she needed. "Three dances would, as you know, send many a tongue wagging and I cannot allow such a thing to happen. I am quite certain you will understand." She lifted her chin, her stomach twisting this way and that in fright as Lord Smithton narrowed his eyes and glared at her.

"My daughter is quite correct, Lord Smithton," Lady Chesterton added, settling a cold hand on Emily's shoulder. "Three dances are, as you know, something that the *ton* will notice and discuss without dissention."

Emily held her breath, seeing how her father and Lord Smithton exchanged a glance. Her eyes began to burn with unshed tears but she did not allow a single one to fall. She was trying to be strong, was she not? Therefore, she could not allow herself to show Lord Smithton even a single sign of weakness.

"I suppose that is to be understood," Lord Smithton said, eventually, forcing a breath of relief to escape from Emily's chest, weakening her. "Given that I have not made my intentions towards you clear, Miss Taylor."

The weakness within her grew all the more. "Intentions?" she repeated, seeing the slow smile spreading across Lord Smithton's face and feeling almost sick with the horror of what was to come.

Lord Smithton took a step closer to her and reached for her hand, which Emily was powerless to refuse. His eyes were fixed on hers, his tongue running across his lower lip for a moment before he spoke.

"Your father and I have been in discussions as regards your dowry and the like, Miss Taylor," he explained, his hand tightening on hers. "We should come to an agreement very soon, I am certain of it."

Emily closed her eyes tightly, feeling her mother's hand still resting on her shoulder and forcing herself to focus on it, to feel the support that she needed to manage this moment and all the emotions that came with it.

"We shall be wed before Season's end," Lord Smithton finished, grandly, as though Emily would be delighted with such news. "We shall be happy and content, shall we not, Miss Taylor?"

The lump in Emily's throat prevented her from saying anything. She wanted to tell Lord Smithton that he had not even asked her to wed him, had not considered her answer, but the words would not come to her lips. Of course, she would have no choice in the matter. Her father would make certain of that.

"You are speechless, of course," Lord Smithton chuckled, as her father grunted his approval. "I know that this will come as something of a surprise that I have denied myself towards marrying someone such as you, but I have no doubt that we shall get along rather famously." His chuckle became dark, his hand tightening on hers until it became almost painful. "You are an obedient sort, are you not?"

"She is," Emily heard her father say, as she opened her eyes to see Lord Smithton's gaze running over her form. She had little doubt as to what he was referring to, for her mother had already spoken to her about what a husband would require from his wife, and the very thought terrified her.

"Take her, now."

Lord Smithton let go of Emily's hand and gestured towards Lady Chesterton, as though she were his to order about.

"Take her to seek some refreshment. She looks somewhat pale." He laughed and then turned away to speak to Emily's father again, leaving Emily and her mother standing together.

Emily's breathing was becoming ragged, her heart trembling within her as she struggled to fight against the dark clouds that were filling her heart and mind. To be married to such an odious gentleman as Lord Smithton was utterly terrifying. She would have no joy in her life any longer, not even an ounce of happiness in her daily living. Was this her doing? Was it because she had not been strong enough to stand up to her own father and refuse to do as he asked? Her hands clenched hard, her eyes closing tightly as she fought to contain the sheer agony that was deep within her heart.

"My dear girl, I am so dreadfully sorry."

Lady Chesterton touched her arm but Emily jerked away, her eyes opening. "I cannot marry Lord Smithton, Mama."

"You have no choice," Lady Chesterton replied, sadly, her own eyes glistening. "I have tried to speak to your father but you know the sort of gentleman he is."

"Then I shall run away," Emily stated, fighting against the desperation that filled her. "I cannot remain."

Lady Chesterton said nothing for a moment or two, allowing Emily to realize the stupidity of what she had said. There was no-one else to whom she could turn to, no-one else to whom she might escape. The only choices that were open to her were either to do as her father asked or to find another who might marry her instead – and the latter gave her very little hope.

Unless Lord Havisham....

The thought was pushed out of her mind before she could begin to consider it. She had become acquainted with Lord Havisham over the few weeks she had been in London and he had appeared very attentive. He always sought her out to seek a dance or two, found her conversation engaging and had even called upon her on more than one occasion. But to ask him to consider marrying her was something that Emily simply could not contemplate. He would think her rude, foolish and entirely improper, particularly when she could not be certain that he had any true affection for her.

But if you do nothing, then Lord Smithton will have his way.

"Emily."

Her mother's voice pulled her back to where she stood, seeing the pity and the helplessness in her mother's eyes and finding herself filling with despair as she considered her future.

"I do not want to marry Lord Smithton," Emily said again, tremulously. "He is improper, rude and I find myself afraid of him." She saw her mother drop her head, clearly struggling to find any words to encourage Emily. "What am I to do, mama?"

"I – I do not know." Lady Chesterton looked up slowly, a single tear running down her cheek. "I would save you from this if I could, Emily but there is nothing I can do or say that will prevent your father from forcing this upon you."

Emily felt as though a vast, dark chasm had opened up underneath her feet, pulling her down into it until she could barely breathe. The shadows seemed to fill her lungs, reaching in to tug at her heart until it beat so quickly that she felt as though she might faint.

"I must go," Emily whispered, reaching out to grasp her mother's hand for a moment. "I need a few minutes alone." She did not wait for her mother to say anything, to give her consent or refusal, but hurried away without so much as a backward look. She walked blindly through the crowd of guests, not looking to the left or to the right but rather straight ahead, fixing her gaze on her goal. The open doors that led to the dark gardens.

The cool night air brushed at her hot cheeks but Emily barely noticed. Wrapping her arms about her waist, she hurried down the steps and then sped across the grass, not staying on the paths that wound through the gardens themselves. She did not know where she was going, only that she needed to find a small, dark, quiet space where she might allow herself to think and to cry without being seen.

She soon found it. A small arbor kept her enclosed as she sank down onto the small wooden bench. No sound other than that of strains of music and laughter from the ballroom reached her ears. Leaning forward, Emily felt herself begin to crumble from within, her heart aching and her mind filled with despair. There was no way out. There was nothing she could do. She would have to marry Lord Smithton and, in doing so, would bring herself more sadness and pain than she had ever felt before.

There was no-one to rescue her. There was no-one to save her. She was completely and utterly alone.

CHAPTER TWO

Three days later and Emily had stopped her weeping and was now staring at herself in the mirror, taking in the paleness of her cheeks and the dullness of her eyes.

Her father had only just now informed her that she was to be wed by the Season's end and was now to consider herself engaged. There had been no discussion. There had been not even a thought as to what she herself might feel as regarded Lord Smithton. It had simply been a matter of course. She was to do as her father had directed, as she had been taught to do.

Emily swallowed hard, closing her eyes tightly as another wave of tears crashed against her closed lids. Was this to be her end? Married to Lord Smithton, a gentleman whom she despised, and allowing herself to be treated in any way he chose? It would be a continuation of her life as it was now. No consideration, no thought was given to her. Expected to do as she was instructed without question – and no doubt the consequences would be severe for her if she did not do as Lord Smithton expected.

A shudder ran through her and Emily opened her eyes. For the first time, a small flickering flame of anger ignited and began to burn within her. Was she simply going to allow this to be her life? Was she merely going to step aside and allow Lord Smithton and her father to come to this arrangement without her acceptance? Was she truly as weak as all that?

Heat climbed up her spine and into her face. Weak was a word to describe her, yes. She *was* weak. She had tried, upon occasion, to do as she pleased instead of what her father had demanded of her and the punishment each time had broken her spirit all the more until she had not even a single thought about disobeying him. It had been what had led to this circumstance. If she had been stronger, if she had been more willing to accept the consequences of refusing to obey her father without question without allowing such a thing to break her spirit, then would she be as she was now?

"Then mayhap there is a time yet to change my circumstances."

The voice that came from her was weak and tremulous but with a lift of her chin, Emily told herself that she needed to try and find some courage if she was to find any hope of escaping Lord Smithton. And the only thought she had was that of Lord Havisham.

Viscount Havisham was, of course, lower in title and wealth than the Marquess of Smithton, but that did not matter to Emily. They had discovered a growing acquaintance between them, even though it was not often that her father had let her alone to dance and converse with another gentleman. It had been a blessing that the requests to call upon her had come at a time when her father had been resting from the events of the previous evening, for her and her mother had been able to arrange for him to call when Lord Chesterton had been gone from the house. However, nothing of consequence had ever been shared between them and he certainly had not, as yet, made his request to court her but mayhap it had simply been too soon for such a decision. Regardless, Emily could not pretend that they did not enjoy a comfortable acquaintance, with easy conversation and many warm glances shared between them. In truth, her heart fluttered whenever she laid eyes upon him, for his handsome features and his broad smile had a profound effect upon her.

It was her only chance to escape from Lord Smithton. She had to speak to Lord Havisham and lay her heart bare. She had to trust that he too had a fondness for her, in the same way that she had found her affections touched by him. Else what else was she to do?

Lifting her chin, Emily closed her eyes and took in a long breath to steady herself. After a moment of quiet reflection, she rose and made her way to the writing table in the corner of the bedchamber, sitting down carefully and picking up her quill.

"Miss Taylor."

Emily's breath caught as she looked up into Lord

Havisham's face. His dark blue eyes held a hint of concern, his smile somewhat tensed as he bowed in greeting.

"Lord Havisham," she breathed, finding even his very presence to be overwhelming. "You received my note, then."

"I did," he replied, with a quick smile, although a frown began to furrow his brow. "You said that it was of the utmost importance that we spoke this evening."

Emily nodded, looking about her and seeing that her father was making his way up the small staircase towards the card room, walking alongside Lord Smithton. Their engagement was to be announced later this evening and Emily knew she had to speak to Lord Havisham before that occurred.

"I know this is most untoward, but might we speak in private?" she asked, reaching out and surreptitiously putting her hand on his arm, battling against the fear of impropriety. She had done this much, she told herself. Therefore, all she had to do was continue on as she had begun and her courage might be rewarded.

Lord Havisham hesitated. "That may be a little...."

Emily blushed furiously, knowing that to speak alone with a gentleman was not at all correct, for it could bring damaging consequences to them both – but for her, at this moment, she did not find it to be a particularly concerning issue, given that she was to be married to Lord Smithton if he did not do anything.

"It is of the greatest importance, as I have said," she replied, quickly, praying that he would consent. "Please, Lord Havisham, it will not take up more than a few minutes of your time." Seeing him hesitate even more, she bit her lip. "Surely you must know me well enough to know that I would not force you into anything, Lord Havisham," she pleaded, noting how his eyes darted away from hers, a slight flush now in his cheeks. "There is enough of a friendship between us, is there not?"

Lord Havisham nodded and then sighed "I am sorry, Miss Taylor," he replied, quietly, looking at her. "You are quite right. Come. The gardens will be quiet."

Walking away from her mother – who did not do anything to hinder Emily's departure, Emily felt such an overwhelming sense of relief that it was all she could do to keep her composure. Surely Lord Havisham, with his goodness and kind nature, would see the struggle that faced her and seek to do what he could to bring her aid? Surely he had something of an affection in his heart for her? But would it be enough?

"Now," Lord Havisham began, as they stepped outside. "What is it that troubles you so, Miss Taylor?"

Now that it came to it, Emily found her mouth going dry and her heart pounding so furiously that she could barely speak. She looked up at Lord Havisham, seeing his features only slightly in the darkness of the evening and found herself desperately trying to say even a single word.

"It is....." Closing her eyes, she halted and dragged in air, knowing that she was making a complete cake of herself.

"I am to be wed to Lord Smithton," she managed to say, her words tumbling over each other in an attempt to be spoken. "I have no wish to marry him but my father insists upon it." Opening her eyes, she glanced warily up at Lord Havisham and saw his expression freeze.

FIND out what happens next between Emily and Lord Havisham in the story available in the Kindle Story A New Beginning

MY DEAR READER

Thank you for reading and supporting my books! I hope this story brought you some escape from the real world into the always captivating Regency world. A good story, especially one with a happy ending, just brightens your day and makes you feel good! If you enjoyed the book, would you leave a review on Amazon? Reviews are always appreciated.

Below is a complete list of all my books! Why not click and see if one of them can keep you entertained for a few hours?

Saved by the Scoundrel
Mending the Duke
The Baron's Malady

The Returned Lords of Grosvenor Square
The Returned Lords of Grosvenor Square: A Regency
Romance Boxset
The Waiting Bride
The Long Return
The Duke's Saving Grace
A New Home for the Duke

The Spinsters Guild
A New Beginning
The Disgraced Bride
A Gentleman's Revenge
A Foolish Wager
A Lord Undone

Convenient Arrangements
A Broken Betrothal
In Search of Love
Wed in Disgrace
Betrayal and Lies
A Past to Forget
Engaged to a Friend

Landon House
Mistaken for a Rake
A Selfish Heart
A Love Unbroken

A Christmas Match
A Most Suitable Bride

Christmas Stories
Love and Christmas Wishes: Three Regency Romance
Novellas
A Family for Christmas
Mistletoe Magic: A Regency Romance
Home for Christmas Series Page

Happy Reading!
All my love,
Rose

JOIN MY MAILING LIST

Sign up for my newsletter to stay up to date on new releases, contests, giveaways, freebies, and deals!

Free book with signup!

Monthly Facebook Giveaways! Books and Amazon gift cards!
Join me on Facebook: https://www.
facebook.com/rosepearsonauthor

Website: www.RosePearsonAuthor.com

Follow me on Goodreads: Author Page

You can also follow me on Bookbub!
Click on the picture below – see the Follow button?

Made in the USA
Middletown, DE
08 April 2021

37220848R00135